Praise for *Not Born of Woman*

"No one but Teel James Glenn could bring us a protagonist quite like private eye Adam Paradise. A giant of a man, with a scarred body and a kind heart, Paradise is the quintessential outsider, and a keen observer of the human condition. He is also a man made from the parts of other men, a literal Frankenstein's monster. Working out of a second-story office, above a drug store in New York City in 1939, Paradise agrees to help a young Romani woman recover a family heirloom. As Paradise works the case, he is confronted by mobsters and Nazis, before coming up against an adversary even more imposing than Paradise himself. Glenn effortlessly crosses and combines genres, respecting and exploiting their tropes, to weave a story that is both familiar and at the same time brand spanking new. *Not Born of Woman* is a thoroughly entertaining read."

- Jeff Markowitz

"In *Not Born of Woman* Teel James Glenn proves a master of pulp crossed-genre mashups full of originality and verve. This book deserves some recognition."

- Lee Murray, multiple Bram Stoker Award® winner and Shirley Jackson Award winner

"Mary Shelley explored philosophical concepts such as the nature of a person in Frankenstein; Teel James Glenn continues this investigation with Frankenstein's monster as a pre-WWII New York City PI. In *Not Born of Woman* Glenn takes us on a mysterious, dangerous adventure full of bad people, occult creatures, and characters we care about—with some important philosophy subtly mixed in. Jump on board with Adam Paradise, a monster with a fedora, to fight the Nazi Bund and learn a bit about your own humanity."

- Carol Gyzander, editor and Bram Stoker Award®-nominated horror author

"An original and ingenious gumshoe epic, *Not Born of Woman* is what would happen if Raymond Chandler and Mary Shelley had a baby that went on to play Sam Spade on the silver screen. The characters jump off the page, and the story moves faster than a bolt of lightning racing down a laboratory lightning rod. Paradise Investigations is going to be the next series everyone is talking about. It's smart, sharp, and authentic, but most of all … it's alive!"

- Nicholas Kaufmann,
bestselling author of *The Hungry Earth* and *The Mind Worms*

NOT BORN OF WOMAN

PARADISE INVESTIGATIONS, BOOK 1

TEEL JAMES GLENN

Copyright © 2024 by Teel James Glenn
ISBN 978-1-63789-127-8
Macabre Ink is an imprint of Crossroad Press Publishing
All rights reserved. No part of this book may be used or reproduced in any manner whatsoever
without written permission except in the case of
brief quotations embodied in critical articles and reviews
For information address Crossroad Press at 141 Brayden Dr., Hertford, NC 27944
www.crossroadpress.com

Cover design by GetCovers

First Edition - 2024

DEDICATION

To Mary Shelley, who was the monster's real mother and who opened the door to worlds on worlds for so many of us.

And to William Henry Pratt, for all the skill in his art and the joy he brought us all.

ACKNOWLEDGMENTS

To my ET, who helps me summon lightning every day, and the writing gang, Nancy, Jaime, Lee, and Wayne, who help bring my writing to life each week. Thanks all.

"What's he that was not born of woman? Such a one am I to fear, or none."

(Macbeth, V, VII, 2-4)

CHAPTER ONE

"You are called Adam Paradise?" The question came from a small woman who hung in the shadows just outside the threshold of my office foyer. She spoke as if she needed permission to enter.

"That's the name I go by," I said as I gestured across my desk to the "client chair" in my office. "Please come in and take a seat."

I set down The *Herald Tribune* newspaper I had been reading, catching up on the problems of the world while I waited for her to overcome her reluctance. The paper was still talking about that Hitler guy in Germany and his influence on the Nazi Bund rally in New York the week before. The First Lady resigned from the Daughters of the American Revolution to protest their refusal to allow negro singer, Marian Anderson, to perform at the DAR's Constitution Hall event in D.C. and in Palestine, thirty-one Arabs were killed in clashes with Jews. In nineteen hundred and thirty-nine years of western civilization, mankind had still not learned to live in peace. Not much had changed in the world since I returned to it.

The woman finally stepped across the threshold and walked, tentatively, through the outer foyer into my office. She sat across from me.

My client chair is set up to put potential customers at ease. It's a soft, big-backed easy chair in a soft blue that is the nicest thing in the room. I had placed it to put the window onto Fifth Avenue at my back. This meant that I was partly in shadow for most of the day if I was sitting at my desk. It hid my scars better.

I also wear gloves because my hands have different-colored skin and textures. My lightly applied makeup ghosted the scarring on my face—though sometimes I just used the excuse of having gone through a car windshield. Some lies have a good purpose.

The new potential client was a dark-haired girl and older than I had thought from the doorway, perhaps in her late twenties but still slender. She also had a slight hunchback that made her seem shorter than she might have been if she stood straight.

Her eyes were wide, searching, and a bit haunted, with black pupils and long lashes. She was dressed in a slightly old-fashioned, plain blue dress with a light cotton jacket just a bit too thin for the February weather. Both were not good fits, as if they were borrowed or hand-me-downs, though they were clean and well maintained. She clearly took pride in her appearance but was not vain.

She wore no makeup and did not need any but did wear large gold hoop earrings and a gold-work necklace that looked eastern European.

A consequence of the unique circumstance of my existence is that I see not only the living but also the essence of those that were once alive. I always have. But as one cannot explain color except as a concept to the colorblind, I cannot fully express how it is that I see this.

Around the woman before me swirled translucent, golden shapes, so I knew this was a person rooted in her heritage and a credit to it, with no dark shadows looming above her.

"They said downstairs in the drug store—" she began.

"Yes," I said, "I don't specify my office is upstairs; just give an address in the phone book. Part of my screening process. How may I help you, Miss—?"

"I am called Vandoma Kalderash."

"Well, Miss Kalderash, why does a *Roma* come to a *gadjo* for help?"

She looked startled. I did my best to smile in as non-threatening a way as possible and added, "I would not be much of an investigator if I could not discover that much about you." This brought an answering, shy smile from her. It looked good on her.

"Leroy, the shoeshine boy outside of Pennsylvania Station, he is a friend of mine," she said. "When Leroy heard of my trouble, he said you might be able to help me. He said you had helped his brother and were a good man. I came because you have no phone."

A good man? Ha, if she knew ….

"Yes, I am old-fashioned and find phones annoying, so I don't have one in the office," I said. "Leroy's brother Jonathan got railroaded on a robbery charge; I uncovered the guy who really did it and got him to … uh … confess." I didn't add that I'd had to break the guy's arm in several places before his conscience kicked in. Usually, just the sight of me was enough for that kind of repentance. One uses what one has to do the job.

"My brother Nico is not so good, sometimes I think," she said haltingly. It was an admission that obviously caused her pain.

"How so?" I sat back to not sound accusing and linked my fingers on my lap to be as non-aggressive as possible.

"He gambles."

The way she said it, I didn't have to be much of a deductive genius to fill in the rest of the story, but I finished, "And he owes money to some bad people?"

I've heard this story more often than not since I set up shop in New York. One of the many things about humanity I've yet to really understand, but I'm trying.

"He owed a lot of money," she continued in barely a whisper, "and so … and so when I was not home, he took from me that which was in my safekeeping and gave the *Kushti Bok* of our family to this man he owed to pay for his losses."

"The good luck of your family?"

Again, the shocked look which made her look older. "You … you speak Romani?"

"I speak a number of languages, Miss Kalderash; it is useful in my work." I'd had much time to learn many things during my long isolation in the Arctic and had continued to learn when I decided to reenter the problematic world of man.

What is existence but to learn and grow?

I was determined to find meaning in the story of my existence and to understand the race of beings called mankind. It is the reason I had assumed my identity—to use my abilities and be fulfilled by being part of the stories of others. New York had been the perfect place to live mostly unnoticed while I quested. "What was this good luck, Miss Kalderash? What does it look like?"

She squirmed a bit then, and I realized how uncomfortable it was for her to reach outside her tribe for help. Much of mankind was still tribal, the Romany even more so than many. That she had come to me showed how desperate she must be.

She was courageous, though, for she continued.

"It was a necklace, much like this." She touched the elaborate but clearly costume necklace she wore. "Though it is of white gold and has a jewel of some size here, so, in the center. A red one, a ruby. It has been in our family for a dozen generations, handed from mother to daughter, and is thought to have much power to bring good." She looked down with shame. "And it is said can also bring much evil."

"Do you know who this man Nico owes?"

"The *gadjo*'s name is Manzetti."

"And how much?"

"It is over a thousand dollars, Mister Paradise." She was having a hard time sitting still, but the words came swiftly now. She leaned forward, wringing her hands together. "This is a very great amount."

"Yet this necklace, as you say, is of gold and has the jewel as well; it is obviously worth much more than that amount of money."

"Yes, this is true in mere money, but worth much, much more to my people. Nico was a *bengalo*, an idiot to take it, to use it this way."

"What is it you want of me? Why have you come to me?"

"I do not have much money," she said. "But if you could talk to this man and ask him to give it back, I promise him in the name of my family to pay him in time all that is owed and more if I must."

"Why can't you talk to him yourself?" I knew what the answer probably was, but I needed her to say it aloud.

"This man, this Manzetti, he does not respect the word of Roma. He says, 'Gypsies are thieves, they are untrustworthy' and such things. This is not true. I do not think he will believe me no matter what I promise."

"And you feel he will believe me?"

Not Born of Woman

"I have asked others about you," she said. "Others besides Leroy. They say, 'Adam Paradise is a man to be trusted; if he gives his word, it will be believed.' I think this is so as well."

"I am complimented, but men like Manzetti will not take the word of anyone. That sort will require some sort of surety."

"I have nothing of value but twenty dollars and my labor," she said. "And the word of a Kalderash." She had a moment of great pride in that name and heritage, then she looked down again with a sudden shame. "I have little to give you but that as well, but—"

"Your word is good enough with me, Miss Kaldarash. Of course, I can make no promise, but if I can do something to recover your Kushti Bok, the fee will be a greater value than money."

She looked at me with sudden uncertainty until I added, "I will accept a home-cooked meal as my fee; it is a long time since I've had one." I had no real need for money with what I had brought back with me from the Arctic; it was not why I had my office and could afford to pursue my assumed profession. And she had a real need.

There was a long pause as she looked at me with a range of expressions from suspicion to confusion but finally, she flew from her chair to race around the desk. She swooped over to give me a hug before I could stop her.

She threw her arms around me, and it was several heartbeats before she truly comprehended how large I was—I felt her slight startled reaction when she did—but her hug did not lessen.

When she stepped away, a little breathless, she looked into my eyes and showed no horror at the scars on my face. And no pity either; that was a first.

I stood up.

Her eyes went a bit wide, but she recovered quickly from the fact that I topped seven feet and towered over her. It was another thing that told me she had courage.

"I do not like them, but they can be useful, so, do you have a phone number I can reach you at?" I asked. I handed a pad of paper and pen to her.

"This is the number of our family home," she said as she wrote on the pad. "My mother does not speak much English—"

"You forget I speak Romani as well as Hungarian."

"Yes," she gave me a shy smile. "She will probably answer if you call—you must not tell her I have come to you with this, that the *Kushti Bok* is gone." She became a little flustered then but recovered again quickly. "You may tell her you are a person for whom I do typing; sometimes I type for writers of the magazines. Piecemeal work."

I took out one of my cards and wrote two phone numbers on the back of it.

"These are the numbers of the phone booths in the candy store downstairs," I said. "Mort is the owner. He will send the boy up with a message if you call. I only give these numbers to clients."

She took the card, her long-fingered hand tiny next to my gloved one.

"You will have the thanks of my heart and my family, Mister Paradise. I will make you a meal to make you burst." Her smile was wide and genuine, and I was determined to find a way to get her necklace back for her.

CHAPTER TWO

The office I rented was on the second floor over a drug store on Fifth Avenue. It was accessed by a steep stairway that disgorged in a shadowed doorway beside the store. I accompanied the girl down and assured her I would call as soon as I had progress of any sort.

I watched Vandoma walk downtown among the midday crowd. She was so small and her coat too light for the weather, yet she seemed in her element. She walked sure and self-contained, negotiating through the rushing bodies, alive and dead, that swarmed around her.

Those shades are not like seeing a projected or even distinct picture of what a person had been; not clearly. They were just shadows of the living beings that had once walked there—phantom shapes like mist or swirling clouds that were what remained when the living had passed on.

Even in the Arctic, I saw the shades of the souls that had died of cold and hunger on that ice-locked ship long before I found it as my refuge. I was always followed by my own swirling mist, now grey, now blue, that I assume were the essences of those who had lived in the bodies from which I had been created.

I cannot speak to nor hear these shades, and I do not know if they are aware of me, indeed if they are aware at all. Perhaps they are only the ashes of those gone, blowing in the wind of the living like so many dead leaves.

All I know is that they are a reality of my world. In the wild places, they are few, but in the concrete canyons of Manhattan, it is like moving through an underwater forest of seaweed with shades all about to a greater or lesser extent. They are never uniform in shape or color; rather, they are amorphous things, translucent and pulsing, that range from black to tinges of white. I conjecture that the events of their life or circumstances of their death influence these factors. However, it is just my conjecture.

Because of this ability, I often went to the motion pictures in an attempt to understand how the naturally living saw the world. Those images on the silver screen—apart from the stories themselves—showed a world unencumbered by the swirling, translucent shapes that were everywhere I looked. Oddly enough, in that dark space that showcased the unreal, I felt more connected to the real world than at any other time.

The golden shapes that hovered over Vandoma seemed to stand apart from the other shades that filled the streets of Manhattan. More personal, even perhaps, protective. Perhaps they too wanted to help her, and the talk that the Rom had a special connection to the spiritual world was the truth.

Newspapers swirled on the streets as well, for it seemed as if March would come in like a lion. The stiff wind that howled down from Canada like a tormented soul forced me to hold onto my hat to secure it but did not bother me much. The arctic wind had been much worse over the long years of isolation, so I'd become inured to the cold. It reminded me of all the seal and polar bear meat I had eaten after my creator left me to die, which made me look forward to Vandoma's home-cooked meal all the more.

I went into Mort's Drug Store, which was directly under my office. To the right was the soda fountain tended by an older teen boy named Jake O'Flynn; to the left was the pharmacy counter where Mort Gluckman, owner of the store, presided over potions and powders. There was a line of magazine and bookracks and several phone booths at the back wall. The phone booths were my destination.

"Hi, Mister P," freckle-faced, red-haired Jake called. A few grey shapes floated above him, but they were faint and faded into the background phantoms that were always around. There were always swirling shapes in the city, and it was never easy to tell if they were specific to the individual or the location. Sometimes it was even overwhelming and confusing for me.

Jake was polishing the counter with great diligence, though more for the reaction it got from the red-haired bobbysoxer sitting sipping an ice cream soda than for doing a good job. She giggled at something he said, and he whispered, "Really, Becky, I saw it!"

I waved at the boy who waved back and to Mort, who was talking with a customer. It is the nature of New York that strangers are quickly accepted in the vast melting pot of the town. It was one of the reasons I chose to make my home there instead of Boston or some other city. In such a place, one could be anonymous and accepted in the small community at the same time.

Along the back wall were racks of pulp magazines—*Weird Tales, Ranch Romances, Argosy, Adventure, The Blue Brother, G 8 and his Battle Aces, Weirdmask, Dr. Shadows, Black Mask,* and many others. They were garishly covered modern mythologies that presented the wish-fulfillment and role models for society.

Two teenage boys were absorbing that mythology, actively debating it as I walked past.

"The Void could take the Spider in a heartbeat," one insisted, pointing at the cover of a black-masked figure with a V slash of a symbol on his faceless mask that proclaimed him 'The Void; He stalks the Soulless!' "You know that Wentworth guy is just nuts, Ron."

"Ain't so, Joey," the other youth insisted. "He didn't seem so nuts in that serial."

"That wasn't really him," Ron shot back. "Just some ham actor."

I passed the boys, and as I did, I heard one whisper, "I bet that guy could pass for Weirdmask. Did you see his kisser?"

"He'd scare The Spider with that face."

I was used to those whispers behind me and the looks that went with them. The tribalism I had observed in mankind often manifests in fear of the other, and I was well aware that I constituted the other to all corners.

When I glanced at the books on the racks that the boys were arguing over, I marveled again at the human need for stories and myths. Was it their self-awareness that caused them to need escape? Was it their own pain that required it or their insecurity at their abilities? Did they need to create behavior to model after to absolve them of making each decision based only on its merits?

I knew that I had so few preconceived notions that often, I was at a loss for a precedent on which to base my decisions. I was my own myth and had none to fall back on.

Those myths that became legends are often the building blocks of civilizations, the unifying force for societies, as well as the causes for division. I had seen much of that of late with the recent rise of the Bund and in the attitude of so many for the so-called "Gypsies"—the Romany, themselves rich in myths of their people.

I squeezed my bulk into the phone booth and called my contact in the police, Lieutenant Tommy Shane, who was always a good conversationalist. I hadn't talked to him since before the Bund rally the week before. Mayor LaGuardia had called out over six hundred officers, Shane included, to cover the Nazi rally at Madison Square Garden. It had been a rough week, and the city had been in turmoil from its spectacle.

"Hi, Adam," he said, "what gets you out of that miserable apartment of yours?" He was one of the few people who had seen the small walk-up apartment on Thirteenth Street in the West Village and knew I had no phone in that building or my office.

"It is not just because I miss beating you at chess," I said. He often stopped by my office for a game, and to be honest, we were about fifty-fifty for games. With me being so much older than him, you'd think I would have the advantage, but he was a very smart cop.

"So, it is business?"

"I'm afraid so," I said. "I was hoping you could stop by the café shift for a little chat when you are off."

"If you're buying, I can," he laughed.

"I think I can handle that," I said. "It won't be long, but I'll bring my portable set."

"I won't have that much time. It's Brendan's recital tonight, but I'll take one of those Italian coffees," he said. "After all, I'm just a poor public servant. Seriously, I'm glad you called. I might have something for you as well."

Not Born of Woman

"Okay, I will see you then."

When I hung up, I noticed Mort had shooed the two boys out, and Jake had finally worked up the courage to chat with bobbysoxer.

"How are you today, Adam?" Mort asked me. He was a stocky man with a thinning halo of silver hair and a perpetual smile.

"Good, Mort. How is business?"

He shrugged. "Meh, good, bad, with the Brownshirts on the streets, I think many people don't want to come out."

"Is it that bad?" I asked. "It seems like there are plenty of people out and about."

Again, he shrugged, this time adding a waggle of his head. "Out and about, maybe, but not coming in."

I looked over at Jake, who was now chatting with his single and rapt female customer. Mort saw my glance and snorted. "That sort of business does not bring in the sheckles."

"Man does not live by bread alone," I quoted. This brought a laugh from him.

"You are an interesting man, Mister Adam Paradise," he said. "A man of many parts."

"That is the truth," I said with a smile. "That is the truth."

Caffe Reggio was on a corner of McDougall Street in Greenwich Village, across town from my apartment and not far from Washington Square Park. It was only about ten years old but already felt like it had been there since the island had been settled. It had a tin roof and paintings on the walls, one of which was from the Caravaggio school. Under it was a bench from a palazzo of the Florentine Medici family.

I often stopped there for a cappuccino and sat quietly to watch the parade of humanity. Tommy and I played chess there as well, so we had both acquired "regular" status in my two years in the city and thus had a table in the back, under the Caravaggio, where we could watch the door.

I was sipping my cappuccino when the burly policeman entered. My friend was a veteran of the Great War and had a slight limp from shrapnel, but it never slowed him down. He was floridly featured, and there was no mistaking his Irish heritage for his red hair and strong jaw. He took off his hat and loosened his scarf.

"I have your cappuccino waiting," I said, rising to shake his hand. He never flinched from my size or features—he topped six feet himself and had seen many horrors in the trenches.

"I do love this Italian coffee," he said as he sipped it.

"Cappuccino," I corrected.

"Yeah, whatever," he mumbled as he gulped it down. He could not grasp that one was supposed to sip and enjoy it. "What did you want to see me about?"

"What can you tell me about a fellow named Manzetti?"

He raised an eyebrow. "You talking about Guido 'Tony' Manzetti, loan shark?"

"That would most likely be the person," I said, "though I didn't know his first name."

"What do you want with him? Taken to betting on the horses?"

"It is gamble enough to cross Fifth Avenue at rush hour," I said. "No, I have a client who has crossed his path."

"Bad business then. He used to work for Big Al here on the east coast before repeal, then went into banking for some of the mob, sort of a neutral moneyman for cash shifts and buyouts. He has a solid reputation for coming through—the sort of guy to hold the money on bets and make sure people pay off. He is somewhere down the food chain from Lepke, but still a big enough fish to put a hurt on people who owe money."

"You saying he had something to do with those two witnesses that were killed last week?" Danny Field and Louis Cohen were two witnesses who agreed to testify against Louis "Lepke" Buchalter before District Attorney Thomas Dewey's Committee on Organized Crime and had been killed before they could appear in court.

Tommy made a tisking sound. "Killing those two was ordered by higher up than him, and word on the street is Kuppy Midgen actually did it, but that's just whispers." He was a good enough cop to know that whispers didn't get convictions.

"That's what I heard," I said, "but I also heard he's vanished unless somebody drops a nickel on him."

"Not likely," he said. "Dewey lost credibility when those two were killed in custody." He said that with the exhausted tone of an honest cop who knew there were some crimes and some criminals beyond his reach and the reach of legal justice. He had the strained look I had often seen on him when the subject of the protected "criminal class" came up. He wanted to have hope for Dewey's reforms but had doubts about any real progress.

It was one of the things I had observed in my time in New York. Most people could accept acts they deemed evil if they did not directly affect them; only a small portion of mankind had the empathy to reach beyond their immediate state to risk themselves for others in jeopardy.

Tommy was such a man, but he had a son and a wife and knew that he could only press against the system so much. I had no such attachments, and so, sometimes, I knew he made use of that.

"What was it you wanted to talk to me about, Tommy?"

He looked away for a moment, and I knew he was going to ask for my help that way again. Since we had met while he was investigating a murder shortly after I arrived in New York, we had collaborated several times on investigations where he had used my outsider status to go where he could not.

"Father Burton, my parish priest, asked me to help him with a parishioner," he said. "I would help him, but I had to fight for time just to see the recital—we are up to our eyeballs with this wave of disappearances. After the chaos of the Bund thing, we are all running on coffee and hope." The way he said it made it clear he did not feel comfortable with the request.

"What's the issue?"

"He was very vague about it," Tommy said. "But it was clear that he needed help but was afraid to ask me directly."

"Like you are now?"

He laughed. "You read people so well, Adam."

"It's my chief hobby."

"Well, that will help with this. Father Burton is a good man and cares about his flock."

"I will talk to him."

"Thank you," he said, still embarrassed by asking me. *So many have trouble asking for help, even Vandoma.* It was one of the many things that made people a mystery to me.

"Is Brendan singing with his chorus tonight?" I asked to bring him out of his ruminations. He smiled immediately.

"Yes," he said. "He has a solo. The show starts at seven. I'm gonna meet Mary there."

"Wow, congratulations," I said. "You better hurry along then to make sure you get a seat up front." We both stood. "Thanks for the information. I'll stop by Father Burton's tomorrow and talk to him."

"Thank you in advance, even if you can't help the Father."

"I'm sure I can do something."

"And watch yourself with Manzetti. Even if he seems incapable of doing anything himself—he delegates, if you know what I mean. He's not that big a fish, Adam, but he's big enough to be trouble," he said. "I hope your client isn't in too deep. He's connected enough to be a problem. Don't think Manzetti is a creampuff, he always has muscle around him."

"Do you really think muscle annoys me?"

Now he laughed. "I suppose not. "He works out of a café in Little Italy. Caffé Algeria."

"Thanks, Tommy."

"Walk softly, big guy," my friend said.

"With size seventeen feet, I don't think so."

CHAPTER THREE

Caffé Algeria, where Guido "Tony" Manzetti held court, was off Mulberry Street in Little Italy, only a short walk from Reggio, so I headed over after Tommy left. It was a storefront with several tables outside where, despite the chill weather, older Italian gentlemen sat, sipped espresso, and ate small cakes while they solved the problems of the world and talked of the good old days.

The old men watched me approach with hooded eyes but were too much New Yorkers to say anything or show any surprise. Clouds of cigarette smoke rose over them and swirled with the breeze as dusk settled over the city. The old men acted as if a seven-foot-tall, dark-haired giant in a leather trench coat and grey Fedora was an everyday thing. It's one of the things I like about New York City.

A little bell over the door rang as I walked in. There was a counter across the room, half a dozen tables with customers seated at them, and a jukebox playing some Caruso record against one wall.

The customers were less circumspect than the old men outside, though they kept their surprise at a stranger entering—even one as unusual as I was—low key. The conversations silenced, and heads turned deliberately away from me, not from fear, but from a need to be able to say "I didn't see nothin'" later on, if things went bad. And it was the kind of place where, I imagined, things did go bad now and then.

Two torpedoes were sitting at a table off to the side, trying to look inconspicuous and failing miserably with the bulges of their holstered guns visible under their poorly tailored suits. Their focus on me was undisguised and immediate.

Manzetti was seated by himself at a table to one side where he had a clear view of the whole room and was pointedly near an exit door that latched on the inside.

He has all his bets covered in case he needs a quick exit.

Manzetti was physically small, a little man, but with a large nose and a balding head. He seemed to be struggling to grow a pencil-thin mustache in the shadow of that nose. His presence was not small, however, when he looked up to fix his dark eyes on me. Those eyes were crystal-clear and showed intelligence behind them.

Swirling shades gathered around him like storm clouds, translucent remnants of many souls that vibrated deep purple and crimson. I felt anger from them, but I couldn't tell whether it was specific to this man or this place. I did know it was from their lives being taken violently. I was used to encountering such things, but the sheer intensity that they projected distracted me for a moment.

Manzetti regarded my moment of hesitation and looked to one of the seated goons with a silent command so that the guy rose and stepped up to block my way. He moved with a predator's grace.

The goon was wide though his head barely came to my collarbone. "I'm here to see Mister Manzetti about some business," I said with a level tone.

"He ain't here to do business with no freak," the goon said. He had stone-cold eyes and a no-nonsense sneer. I will give credit to him that he was not the least cowed by my appearance.

His mistake.

I shot out my right hand and gripped his throat faster than he could grab for his gun or my arm. I lifted him off the floor with casual strength and looked down at Manzetti even as the other torpedo jumped to his feet and drew his own pistol.

The gunman could not fire his gun at me, however, as I made sure if he shot at me, he was endangering his boss in the direct line of fire.

Manzetti, unruffled, took a puff of his cigarette and regarded me with a stoic expression. After a few moments, he blew smoke out of his large nose and sighed.

"I am called Adam Paradise; I have money business for you, Mister Manzetti. Do we talk?"

Not Born of Woman

"Let that boob Mickey down and try not to break him. Take a seat," he said. "But it better be worth my time."

I set Mickey down without looking back at him and sat across from the loan shark, watching the two torpedoes in the reflective surfaces of the tin walls behind Manzetti. They stood staring at me with confused expressions for a few beats before returning to their seats.

The conversations of the rest of the customers went back to a normal level, but I could feel their sidelong glances.

"Talk, big man," the gangster said in a low, harsh whisper that carried an implied threat.

"A man named Nico Kalderash owes you money from some gambling losses. He gave you a family heirloom as surety on that debt. I want to redeem it for him and pay his debt in full."

"The Gypsy is a loser, pal. All gamblers are losers, they oughta know the house always wins." He sipped his espresso, took a long drag on his cigarette again, and then grinned. It was an expression that didn't suit his face well. "But Nico is a bigger loser than most. He's got that monkey on his back really bad. You're throwing money down a hole to bail him out, he's a lost soul."

"No soul is truly lost," I said. "None, in any case, that is cared for, and Nico has those who care for him."

"Like you?"

"By proxy."

"You got big steel ones, buddy. What makes you think I'll give you the dingus?"

I was aware that the two torpedoes were leaning forward in their chairs on the balls of their feet and ready for a call to action.

"You are a smart man, a businessman, sir." I said, "I am offering you a profit on the necklace. I will give you ten percent over the value you are holding it for, and everyone can be happy."

"You think my purpose in the world is to make people happy?"

"'*The most intelligent men, like the strongest, find their happiness where others would find only disaster,*'" I quoted. "It is better to bring happiness than disaster."

He laughed derisively. "You think your little carnival act with Mickey is impressive? You think that tough face of yours means anything to me?"

"I don't think I really mean anything to you, but it doesn't matter if you want to do business. Cash money. Here and now. I thought that was the way you liked to work."

"Let me tell you, tall mister," he said, leaning forward to stare me directly in the eyes. His voice was a death rattle whisper. "No matter how tough your face is, there is a baseball bat built to fit."

I let myself give a short laugh. "So, you don't have it then. Who did you sell it to?"

This startled him, and he sat back. "How—?"

"If you had it, sir, you would have tried to jack the price up over the ten percent. Quite a bit, I suspect, as a matter of course. I'll pay a finder's fee of fifty dollars to tell me who you sold it to."

He slapped the table, and everyone else in the room jumped.

His torpedoes came to their feet before they realized Manzetti was laughing.

"Yup, balls of steel," he snorted and crushed out his cigarette. "Okay, big man, put down the money, a hundred dollars."

I reached into my coat—slowly so as not to excite the two gunmen—and withdrew a hundred dollars which I set on the table. He nodded as if I had confirmed his opinion of me.

"I sold the Gypsy trinket to Otto Dorfman uptown. He runs a pawnshop on Eighth Avenue in Chelsea and maybe a couple of other businesses on the side. Don't know how he knew I had it, but he came to me and offered twice what the kid owed me. I told the kid the same thing."

"Nico tried to get this back?"

"Last night," the Italian said. "But he didn't have cash up front, so I had Mickey show him the door."

"You are a very smart businessman, Mister Manzetti."

"Don't think I'm not, pal. Or a soft touch."

"Not a mistake anyone could make, sir."

"Not twice, anyway," he added. "But you will owe me after this."

"Owe you?"

Not Born of Woman

"The vig isn't always money, Mister Paradise."

I stood up. "Thank you for your businesslike manner, Mister Manzetti."

I made it to the door while keeping an eye on Mickey and a nearby partner, both of whom stared daggers at me. Mickey walked to open the door for me with a cold smile on his lips.

"I'll remember you, pal." The purple wraiths that swirled around him were very specific; there was a clear miasma of death about this man. The phantoms of the dead had unfinished business with him.

"It would do for you to forget me," I suggested in a genial tone to the thug. "I've been known to induce nightmares."

"I'll bet, Frankenstein," he said. "We'll talk about it when I see you again."

I almost said something harsh but restrained myself and said simply, "As you wish. Have a good day."

I was aware of him staring as I departed and was pretty sure he would have shot me in the back if it would not have inconvenienced his employer to have a commotion. I did not feel entirely out of danger until I was well down the block.

I really do hate it when they call me by my creator's name; I blame that Karloff fellow.

CHAPTER FOUR

Father David Burton was a small man with a fringe of silver hair that put me in mind of the druids from which the Catholic Church appropriated the tonsure. He received me in his second-floor study in the rectory to his church on Fifteenth Street off Sixth Avenue.

He did a good job of not being off-put by my appearance, accepting me as he would any parishioner—that in and of itself was remarkable but all the more so because it was a record; twice in two days, a stranger accepted me as I was. Or maybe I was getting better at my "I'm harmless" expressions.

"As much as I appreciate you coming here, Mister Paradise, I don't understand why Tommy sent you to me." The priest spoke in a quiet tone that was at odds with his manner.

He was seated behind his desk, which was filled with paperwork. Around him, the translucent essence of the dead flowed, all golden and glowing, and I assumed it meant they were at peace with their passing. I had seen such before around some holy men and women who had attended the dying as if the essence of those who died was bonded to them in some way.

"I have no current needs," the priest continued. "I think Tommy is being a worry-wort."

The priest was not a good liar. There was a grimness about him, a downcast bearing of his being, as if a great weight rested on his shoulders and the corners of his mouth worked a bit too hard to be genial.

Not Born of Woman

He also looked down at his paperwork when he spoke, then up with that artificial smile that I am sure appeared genial to his parishioners but did not fool me at all. I think in poker they call it a tell.

"I don't think Tommy is prone to hysteria, Father," I said. "I'm sure you're in some sort of trouble, and I only offer to help if you want me to."

He looked away again and his brow wrinkled in discomfort. "Are you a Catholic, Mister Paradise?" He looked directly at me. "Though Tommy has mentioned you in a professional sense he has never elaborated."

"My beliefs are catholic in their nature," I said, "though my religion is not so specific."

"You sound like a politician."

"'He that will believe only what he can fully comprehend must have a long head or a very short creed.'"

"That is a quote," he said perking up with interest. "Father Teilhard de Chardin?"

"The French Jesuit, yes. I find his contrasts and connections of religion and science insightful."

"Unusual reading for a private detective."

"I prefer investigator," I said with no animosity. "It has a broader definition."

"Then your broad reading should have told you that the seal of the confessional is absolute."

Here was the problem; he'd heard something in the confessional that so bothered him he almost broke his vow to ask for help from Tommy, but now had thought better of it and was shying. The question was how to get around his reluctance. Devout men can be stubborn, to say the least.

"And what I wished to speak to Tommy about was—uh—it concerns something I cannot speak about." He stood up to look out the window at the street beyond, apparently unable to face me while he lied. "I was premature in contacting him; I must speak with my bishop on this."

The shades that hovered near the priest changed color now to a muted rust, tinged with gold as if to reflect his turmoil. "I regret that you have taken time from your day for this wasted trip."

"'The most satisfying thing in life is to have been able to give a large part of one's self to others,'" I quoted.

He turned back to look at me and his lips gave a slight curl despite his gloom. "Now you school me with quotes from the Jesuit?"

"By no means," I said. "I merely point out that this is no great trouble for me to come by. Tommy is a good friend."

He was affected by that and I could see the play of his emotions as he wrestled with whether to open himself to me with his problem. In that long moment where he thought about it, I noticed the swirling shades that hovered over him began to deepen in color sliding toward dark purple shot through with angry flashes of gold and yellow.

I had never seen that before, where the remembered essence reacted in real-time to the human they swarmed around. I felt a strange chill as I saw this and with some premonition, I suddenly felt I had to act.

I sprang over the desk in a move so swift that I caught the priest between breaths and slammed into him to knock him down from the window at the same moment the glass windowpane exploded inward.

We both toppled to the ground as shards from the window showered over us, followed by three sharp cracks.

"Mother of Mercy!" Burton yelled when he could breathe.

"Stay down, father," I hissed and peeked up at the edge of the window. I just barely saw a shape across the street. It was someone at the building under construction.

"What happened?" Father Burton gasped as my weight rolled off him.

"Those were gunshots, Father," I said. I rose and saw the vague shape darting away. He was too far for me to even consider chasing him.

"Gunshots?" He was shaking from my physical assault and judging by his expression had a hard time comprehending the violence he had just avoided.

Not Born of Woman

"Yes, father," I said. I closed the curtains to darken the room and pulled him, unresisting, away from the window into the hall outside the office. "Are you still going to insist there is no reason for Tommy or me to be of use to you? That there is nothing wrong?"

He could not find words to deny it now, knowing his lie had been found out, so he just stared sheepishly at me.

I pulled the phone off his desk, dialed the police precinct, and had them put me through to Tommy.

"What can I do for you, Adam?" he said in a hurried voice. "I'm really up to my armpits on the missing girls' case."

"You need to get over to Father Burton's, Tommy, someone just tried to kill him."

"What!?"

"They took a couple of shots with a rifle through a window. He's fine, but you'd better get over here fast."

"Stay with him!" He hung up and I imagined him racing out the door.

I turned to the priest who was now composing himself. "Do you want to tell me what you learned in the confessional that would compel someone to want to kill you?"

He shook his head. "I am sorry, Mister Paradise. I do appreciate what you've done for me here today, but I must keep my covenant with my God, and I'm afraid I cannot say anymore."

"Are you sure you weren't the target, Adam?" Tommy asked me while the crime lab team went over the office and swarmed around the construction site across the street.

"Do you really think someone could miss me three times?" I asked. We were standing on the street in front of the rectory. Tommy was smoking with an intensity that was almost angry.

"That is a little hard to imagine, big guy, but why could anyone want to shoot a priest?" His faith was deep, and the thought of the attack alone was upsetting to his worldview. For all the dark side of humanity his police position afforded him he still had a lot of hope in his heart. "If he heard something in the confessional, he couldn't possibly tell anyone. It is a sacred promise."

"Not everyone believes in that kind of honor, Tommy," I said. "But it presents a real problem; how do you protect a man who will not admit—even after this—that he needs to be protected? And who cannot even provide a clue for us to follow?"

Tommy blew out smoke with a deep sigh. "There are enough fellows at the precinct that we can keep someone with him around the clock to protect him, at least for a while. They'll do it on their own time."

"But for how long?" I asked. "You said yourself that with the rash of disappearances you're pushing overtime as it is."

"I know," he said, "But the boys will do this on their own time; I'm not going to even ask the commissioner, at least until there is something solid to present as a case."

"So, it's on me?" I laughed.

He grinned. "I'm afraid so."

"Well, I was the Johnny on the spot, so it's personal for me now as well."

"Thank you," he said sincerely. "I'll give you any help I can."

"I know."

The crime lab team exited the rectory and the chief technician walked up to us.

"What's the word, Clancy?" Tommy asked the overweight, balding scientist.

Clancy gave a sidelong glance at me. I wasn't sure if it was my look or that I was not on the force, but it was clear he was reluctant to speak in front of me.

"It's okay," my detective friend said. "He's on our side."

The technician seemed about to say something but was too much of a worker bee to complain. "They were nine-millimeter slugs, Detective Shane. Two were deformed but one of them went into some plaster and we should be able to get some striations on it—so if we can find the gun, we can match it."

Not Born of Woman

"Any idea what type of gun?" Tommy asked.

"We found casings over in the construction site. My guess is a European semi-automatic. Maybe a Mauser or Bayard. I'll know more when we put the casings under the microscope."

"Not a rifle?" I asked.

"No," he said. "Maybe a full-length pistol, but not a sniper rifle."

"That meant the shooter was a damn good shot to make that hit from across the street," I said.

"I understood he missed," Clancy said. From the way he looked at me he was having a hard time imagining anyone missing a target my size.

"Well," I said, "Nobody's perfect."

"Thanks, Clancy," Tommy said. "I'll see you back at headquarters."

After the man left, my friend turned to me. "I'm going to try one more time to see if I can get anything from Father Burton, but I don't think that is going to lead anywhere."

"I agree with you on that. He is, as they say, committed to silence. So, it's up to me."

"You've got broad shoulders, big guy," he said.

"'It is our duty as men and women to proceed as though the limits of our abilities do not exist.'" I quoted de Chardin again.

"You're something special, Mister Paradise," he said.

"You have no idea, Tommy. But thank you."

CHAPTER FIVE

The pawnshop run by Otto Dorfman was on Eighteenth Street at Eighth Avenue just across town from Father Burton's rectory, so I walked directly there after saying goodbye to my friend. I promised I would let Tommy know of anything I uncovered about the priest's situation.

I had asked Tommy if he knew anything of Dorfman and he'd said there were whispers the man was a fence, which made sense that Manzetti would deal with him, but the question was how had Dorfman known the necklace was with the Italian? And why did he want it so badly?

Dorfman's establishment was one of several pawnshops on that avenue and had little to distinguish it from the others save that somehow it seemed a bit shabbier. It was hard to judge that, in so much as they all had the traditional pawnbroker's signs out front. Those three globe signs were thought to originate in the Italian region of Lombardy, where pawnshop banking originated under the name of Lombard banking. The three-sphere symbol was long attributed to the Medici family of Florence, Italy, owing to its symbolic meaning in heraldry. They were originally coins but became the spheres to better advertise.

Dorfman's store had pretty much the same written signs as the other places as well: "storage loans made on clothing and furs during the summer months," bargains in luggage, trunks, wardrobe, sporting goods, and a Holmes electric protection sign but they were faded and more weathered. The brilliant colors of the other stores gave way to faded paint and bleached-out banners on Dorfman's.

Not Born of Woman

The wares in the window display were the usual assortment of pipes, gold cigarette cases, watches, and assorted jewelry, but no Romani necklace.

The thing that stood out about the shop was that while the two stores on either side of Dorfman's were open for midday business, his was still locked up. That was puzzling because New Yorkers opened early and closed late in an attempt to get the jump on the next guy.

I got a cup of coffee in a small diner across the street from the store and watched the store for a bit to decide my next move.

I had little or nothing by way of a clue as to the priest's antagonist save that I had to assume it was someone who had attended confession. I would have to canvas his neighborhood and observe his flock, which would take some time.

Meanwhile, I had a chance to retrieve Vandoma's *Koshti Bok* whenever Dorfman finally opened.

The day wore on and I was forced to order lunch to keep from drawing more attention to myself—well, more attention than I usually get. I ate slowly while keeping an eye on the storefront.

It gave me time to study the habits of those who were forced by circumstance to bring their valuables to men like Manzetti or Dorfman. Even with the Depression slowly fading in the world, there was still a need for people in sore straits to have cash, and pawnshops were a source of that ready cash, especially during the holidays. The desperate brought in items of value and exchanged them for money.

The shops held the items for a state-mandated period, during which the customers could reclaim their property by paying back the loan plus interest. After that, the pawnbroker was free to sell them and keep the profit, but few I saw enter seemed to be shopping for bargains. Those whom I observed entering the other pawnshops all did so with haggard looks, shoulders hunched, and heavy steps. Money flowed from the shops into threadbare pockets while family memories, mementos, and jewelry were left behind.

Pawnbrokers were strictly regulated with a criminal background check and permits renewable annually so Tommy's suspicion about Dorfman being a fence for stolen goods would certainly explain Manzetti doing business with him. Technically, buying from Manzetti meant he had not committed a crime in this case, but it was on the borderline since Nico had left it for surety and had not actually sold it to the gangster.

I'd learned from looking through the phonebook that old Otto lived in an apartment above the shop and so, after I could not bear any more refills on the tepid coffee, I decided to see if he was sleeping in that day.

I made my way across the street through the post-lunch crowd just as a cold, light drizzle started. It worked to my benefit as it cleared many from the streets and gave me an excuse to huddle in the doorway that was the entrance to the apartment above the store. It was a deep, shadowed doorway so there was no difficulty hiding myself as I worked on gaining entrance with a set of lock picks.

For a man who handled valuables regularly, his choice in locks was very poor as I was able to pick the lock in mere moments. Inside was the same sort of narrow staircase that I had leading to my office over Mort's store. The lights were off. I decided not to flick the switch and went as quietly up the stairs as possible.

I was now officially breaking and entering. It was the other major difference between Tommy and me; he had to obey the law, and I was only interested in justice. And since my identity was arbitrary and my investigator's license bogus to begin with, I had little fear of their loss if minor violations accomplished my ends.

I would be sad to move to another city and assume another identity for the friends I had made, but my purpose was to learn as much about humanity as I could. I had no idea how long my life would be since I had no peers to measure it against, so a move would be just another adventure.

The door at the top of the stairs was also equipped with only a cheap lock but, disturbingly, it was ajar.

I stopped and listened.

There were no noises of life from inside the apartment, but there was the faintest purple glow from beyond the portal.

I gently pushed the door in and peered into the darkened room.

Inside the railroad apartment looked like a tornado had hit it—chairs overturned, their undersides ripped up, the couch slit into fragments, drawers pulled out of all the bureaus. And right in the middle of the room, lying on his face, was a body I was pretty sure had belonged to Otto Dorfman.

All this was illuminated by the amorphous essence of the no longer living being that lay there, glowing purple and black as it hovered over the corpse, pulsing with angry streaks of crimson that proclaimed he'd died violently.

I crept into the room with soft steps, senses alert. A few feet into the room the smell of death hit me, that pungent, bitter scent of decay that was so ironically much stronger from human death than any other animal. It was almost overwhelming.

There was no need to check the body, no doubt he had been dead for at least a day from the smell.

I paused in the center of the room to take it all in.

The purple phantom shape was the only light, but it was a violently bright and angry mist floating over its former host form. I could see a bullet hole in the left temple of the fallen man, who had been a thin middle-aged man with a close beard and a long thin nose. His eyes were wide and staring in a final expression of horror.

Looking at the contorted position of the body, my eyes were drawn to his hands that were bound behind his back. All his fingers jutted out at odd angles. They had been systematically broken; he had suffered for a long time before his misery ended with a bullet through his brain.

Mankind had a capacity for violence that still startled me—the animal kingdom could be savage, but it was savagery in the heat of combat, in the quest for survival. Man was the only being I knew of that made the suffering of others an art form.

But did he discover them while they were searching, and they tortured him to find out—what? And did he tell them what they wanted to know, and they killed him anyway? Did he know them and could identify them?

I moved gingerly around the room, looking carefully among the chaos, and found what the searches may have been looking for: a safe hidden behind a breakfront that had been overturned. The safe that had been concealed behind it was now wide open.

I had a small flashlight in my trenchcoat pocket and used it to look in the safe. There were a few trinkets still left in it, some earrings, a tray of rings with precious stones in it, and some ledger books.

So, they did not want jewelry. At least not this jewelry.

As I was wearing gloves, I felt no problem with slipping the ledger out. A quick look confirmed what I had suspected; it was a record of transactions by the dead man that I suspected were not on the up and up.

It was all in code, of course, or at least in initials to names I did not have a clue about, but they were dated entries, so I skipped ahead to the last couple of days. There it was: GM—1,300 dollars—Nec. (to r.s. to N'z? Jack up!).

GM had to be Guido Manzetti and nec had to be Necklace.

But r.s.? *Resale?*

And "N'z" would not mean anything to me but for the fact that there was a Swastika next to that notation.

I glanced down at the dead man again. "Really, Otto?" I said out loud. "Selling to the Bund boys? Why would they want a Romani artifact?" I noticed then that there was a spent cartridge near him, so it was likely a semi-automatic that had killed him.

I looked back through the notations and found three other swastika marks near a: cross, b: relic, c: Hopi Kachina.

"Different cultures, different religions," I said. "What were you doing, Otto?"

Of course, the late pawnbroker could not answer me, but I thought I detected a ripple of dark color in the floating mass over him. *Perhaps the newly dead still had some connection to the living world?*

I put the ledger back exactly as it had been and retraced my steps to the door, careful to leave no trace of my passage. I wondered if my search for the *Koshti Bok* was over, that perhaps Nico had somehow figured out to whom Manzetti had sold that necklace. Had the Roma been desperate enough to perpetrate this outrage to rectify his family mistake?

It was hard to imagine Vandoma's kin being so different from her, but I had come to see that humans were capable of great variation in personality and beneath the civilized surface often lurked the beast.

I hope not.

Not Born of Woman

I pulled the door to, exactly as I had found it, then went back downstairs and out onto the street to a payphone where I dropped a nickel in.

"Sorry to call again so soon, Tommy," I said when I got my friend on the phone, "but I'm afraid I have a little more business for you." I then told him that I'd found the downstairs and upstairs doors both ajar (a little white lie about one of them) and said I'd only looked in, seen the body, and then come down to call.

"You are a trouble magnet, Adam," he said to me with no real accusation. He called across the squad room and told his sergeant to get the car ready and to call the crime lab again. "Wait by the door downstairs, Adam, and I'll meet you there."

"Will do." I hung up and contemplated what was next.

It was now clear that Vandoma's necklace was something special if, among all the things in that ledger, it was grouped with the other articles. But Nazis? It seemed that they were everywhere of late.

I huddled in the doorway and tried to think of what to tell the Romani girl. "Hi, I'm afraid your family heirloom was sold to a criminal and then stolen. No, I don't have any clue that I can follow to find it."

Nope, I can't do that.

That left me having to come up with some avenue to pursue.

It meant that now I had to find Otto Dorfman's killer.

The day was getting busy.

CHAPTER SIX

I was occupied for a little more than an hour with Tommy and his team and had to pull all my personal influence with my friend to keep from being taken down to the station right then and there to fill out witness reports for both incidents.

"Okay, Adam," he finally said, "but you better show up early tomorrow and be prepared to recite chapter and verse or I'm gonna lose points with my boss."

"Scout's honor," I said with a smile. "I'll be there ready to sing like a seraph."

He snorted. "Fallen one," he said. "Okay, off with you and try not to stumble onto any more police business before tomorrow. I gotta have some time at home, my wife has almost forgotten what I look like."

I promised the impossible and headed out contemplating the one new fact I'd gleaned after the crime scene investigators had gone through the apartment and released the body. The bullet casing that had been left was from a nine-millimeter, probably a Banyon or Mauser—exactly the same kind of weapon used to fire at Father Burton.

We would know for sure when the slug was recovered from inside Otto's head.

And my initial guess had been correct; all his fingers had been broken individually before he was murdered. Most likely to force the combination of the safe from him once it had been discovered.

Not Born of Woman

It was dark as night at only four in the afternoon with the rain a full-fledged downpour, but I was glad for it. It cleaned the streets of both dirt and people and gave me a respite from curious stares.

I passed the marquee of a movie theatre where people huddled under the overhang against the rain, though it was early for the dinner show of the features.

I smiled when I saw it was advertising the *Son of Frankenstein* film that came out the month before "held over for matinees" while it announced a coming musical remake of *The Three Musketeers* with someone called the Ritz Brothers.

I was struck again by how both much and yet how little mankind had progressed since my creation; empires had fallen and risen, man had learned to fly and drove around in autos, but the cruel delusions of grandeur that had surrounded my creation almost two hundred years before was still part of the daily world.

Here it was 1939 and I still was searching for my place in it. I had become a half-remembered myth turned amusement fiction trying to find my place in the grand scheme—if indeed there was one. At the moment, my search for purpose had me trying to help a Romani woman and I was failing miserably at it.

I felt I had to call my client to keep her apprised of my progress or lack of it, but before I called Vandoma I wanted to know more about this necklace that was so important it was a hot potato of interest to a killer and a bunch of organized racists playing soldiers.

The question in my mind when I left Tommy was, why would the Nazis want a Romani necklace? *It could not have had that much gold in it, and from Vandoma's description, the jewel was not very large.*

It seemed Nico was unlikely to have so desperate a reason that he would resort to violence, but I needed to know for sure.

Whenever I had a question for almost anything, I went to the best-kept secret in the city, The Tome Tomb, a little bookstore on book row—Third Avenue in the Twenties under the rumbling shadow of the elevated train. It was an overcrowded hole-in-the-wall place, with books stacked to the ceiling and every conceivable nook jammed full of rare and out of print books.

The resource, however, was the proprietor himself, "Digger" Tome—a little gnomish man who used to have a memory act at a carnival because he had a photographic mind and was a voracious reader of everything. It made him a collector of odd facts and better than a visit to the New York Public Library when one wanted to research almost anything.

I arrived at his store right near closing time, dripping wet. The store was empty and there was a jazz tune playing on a radio on a shelf behind Digger when I entered.

"How're you doing, Eclipse?" He called to me without looking up from the funny book he was reading. He reached behind him and turned the tune down to a whisper. "'Without music, life for me would be a mistake,'" he said with an expectant tone.

"Nietzsche," I said, and he gave a short snort that was his laugh.

It was a game we played, our own form of mental chess, so I replied. "'We are such stuff as dreams are made on, and our little life is rounded with a sleep.'"

It was good there were no other customers in the narrow store since I had to stand sideways to fit in the space without my shoulders knocking books down. I often came to his store for books, as I am a voracious reader as well, but I think there was more information in his head than on the shelves.

"*The Tempest*, act four, scene one," he said without hesitation. "What can I do for you?" He sat behind a high counter, hunched over the funny book. He wore thick glasses, his skin pasty white, thinning hair plastered to his head, and I realized that in the three years I had been in the city I had never seen him step out from behind the counter. I began to wonder if he ever went out into the sunlight at all.

"I'm looking for any reason why the Bund members here in the city would want a Kachina doll, a cross, and an antique Romani necklace."

I saw his eyes widen and he looked up from the comic book. "Bund? Those Nazi jerks?" He looked like he had licked a lemon. "You getting mixed up with them?"

"Not as a client," I said to reassure him. "But my path looks like it is going to cross theirs." That appeased him and his features became thoughtful.

Not Born of Woman

"Any specific cross or Kachina doll?" he asked. "There is a whole world of Hopi/Navajo Deities to choose from."

"No idea."

"And just saying a cross does not narrow things down."

"Sorry," I said. "But I can give you more on the necklace."

"What tribe of Roma?"

"The family is Kalderash."

He stared off into space for a long moment. I thought for a second that I had stumped him but then he gave a little grin and when he spoke it was like he was reading off a page—he probably was—of something he had read a decade or more ago.

"Kalderash, originally a Romanian name, but some of that tribe were also from Hungary. From the Latin *caldare*—or cauldron. Probably from tinkers or jewelry makers."

"Yes, but—"

He held up a finger to silence me as I saw him mentally turning pages. "There is a legend of a *Kushti Bok*, or a good luck charm, created in 1683 in celebration of the defeat of the Ottoman Armies in the Battle of Vienna that ended their rule over Transylvania and when Roman Catholicism became the official religion. It is rumored to have helped cause the defeat to make the owner and wearer quote 'mighty,' unquote."

"So, it has no great intrinsic value?" I asked, "I mean, money-wise?"

"It might have some historical value," Digger said. "Just the age alone gives it that and it has considerable cultural significance. And certainly, to the Romani themselves, it has great value. Other than that, the gold in it does not have a lot of value, and the jewel is not so big from what I recall reading. A ruby, I think. I am sure I've seen a picture of it in a book but will have to search." I was sure he meant in his mental archives.

"Yes. But why would the Bund boys want it?"

"It's been rumored that the paperhanger over there in Europe is nutty for the occult, fortune-telling, and talismans of every sort, Spear of Destiny, Tibetan Relics, Saint's blood, etcetera." He turned the page in his comic book, looked down at it then up at me, blinking like an owl. "The other two things, the Indian doll and any number of crosses, as you know are considered to have magical powers by their respective religions. If they thought the Kalderash necklace really had some effect on or caused the Ottoman's defeat that might be reason enough for them to want it. Who wouldn't want to be mighty?"

I considered this for a moment. "Do you think there's anything to it?"

"I suppose it doesn't matter if it did or not if they believe it did, right?"

"Yes, I suppose everything is a matter of personal belief," I said. "It's what has compelled most of mankind forward, is it not?"

"'There are no facts, only interpretations,'" he said.

"Nietzche, again," I said. "He seemed to understand some of the deeper aspects."

"You're not going to be tangling with these Nazis, Adam, are you?"

"I don't know, Digger." I said honestly. "I'm on a case that seems to have butted up against them so I may have to."

"Just be aware of something else that Nietzche said: 'He who fights with monsters might take care lest he thereby become a monster.'"

I suppressed a laugh. "I will do my best to resist the urge. I'll try to keep things logical and make sense of it all."

He held up the comic book to show me the panels of a guy in red and blue tights with a red cape. "They make about as much sense as this stuff," he said with a grin. "Them bent cross boys believe in all sorts of weird stuff, death rays, heck, even talk about making their own super soldiers out of dead people." He laughed.

I laughed in sympathy. "Yeah," I said. "What a silly idea."

There was no putting it off, I had to talk to Vandoma, if only to keep her apprised of my lack of progress, though I was hoping she might be able to give me some kind of lead. I had to also broach the subject of talking to her brother directly.

Not Born of Woman

"Hello, Kalderash residence." The voice of the woman who answered was an older one and from those few words, it was clear English was not her first language.

"Good evening, Mrs. Kalderash," I said in Hungarian. "Is Vandoma there? I am Adam Paradise. She is doing some typing for me."

She showed no surprise at the message and called to her daughter. In a few moments, the girl's pleasant voice spoke.

"Mister Paradise," she said with hidden hope in her tone. "It is good to hear your voice."

"And yours, Miss Kalderash." I added quickly, "But I do not have much in the way of progress to report." I could hear her let out her breath in a little sigh.

"What can I do for you, sir?" she reverted to a formal tone, and I could picture her mother standing nearby overseeing.

"I realize you can not speak freely, but there have been complications—Manzetti sold the necklace to a third party—"

She gasped so I rushed to continue. "Do not worry, I will keep working to get it back for you, but I think I will need to speak to Nico directly about this. Can you arrange that?"

"I ... uh, think so—where?"

"I have an appointment in the morning. Do you think you could get him to my office after lunch tomorrow, around, say, two?" I didn't mention my worries that Nico might have visited Dorfman, but I would put that to her brother directly.

"I do not know—"

"If you have to, tell him I have a job for him to keep the fiction that you are picking up typing from me. Okay?"

"I can do that," she said, adding, no doubt for her mother's benefit, "I will come by to pick up the manuscript from your office around two if that will be sufficient?"

"Good," I said. In an attempt to leave her with hope and lighten the mood I added, "I expect an A-one meal in a couple of days, Miss Kalderash. My mouth is watering for it already."

She laughed with a lightness I had not imagined still existed in the world. "You have the stomach of a Romani, Adam Paradise."

This made me smile, for, in truth, I did.

Teel James Glenn

It was one of the gifts from my creator ....

CHAPTER SEVEN

The rain was a memory as I walked across town to my apartment. The streets were filled again, as the denizens of New York seemed to thrive in the night and a chill damp wind was not going to confine them.

My apartment was on West Thirteenth Street down the block from Church of the Village, at Seventh Avenue, and a block off from St. Vincent's Hospital. The hospital served a wide range of New Yorkers in this neighborhood so full of poets, writers, artists, homeless people, the poor, and the working class. It had served for many years through plague and war and had been a refuge for the outsiders of the city.

Mine was a block with three- and four-story red brick buildings, some of them with clinging vines that spoke of their age. Many of them had stoops while some had step-down entrances. All had a quaint quality to them, a feeling of individuality and craftsmanship. Much of the West Village was the same way and it reminded me of a European village plunked down in the midst of the big city's skyscrapers. It made me feel a little closer to my birth time and place.

My apartment was a three-floor walk up to a roof penthouse studio with a large Northeast-facing window. The floor-to-ceiling window allowed the room to fill with light each morning and gave me a clear view of the new Empire State Building. That massive modern Tower of Babel was a monument to the technological progression of mankind; if only the moral level of man could keep up.

That night, as on many, the sounds of musicians playing drifted out open windows and reminded me of the streets of Marseille or of

Geneva, both places I had passed through on my way to this new world.

As I approached my door, I became aware that footsteps matching mine came from behind me. Several people seemed to be following me.

I slowed my steps and crossed the street as if I was going to a different address, to see if my suspicion was correct. My stalkers matched my moves which removed any doubt that they were in pursuit of me.

The question was why? Who would have reason to shadow me?

I had not had any active investigations for several weeks. Now Vandoma's case and the Father Burton problem were all that occupied me, though no one could have known of my involvement with the priest since it was so recent.

I could not imagine simple street thugs would chance their hand against someone my size or aspect. Therefore, they had reason to pursue me. I decided I wanted to know what that reason was.

At the corner of Eighth Avenue, I turned and stopped abruptly in the shadow of a building. And waited.

The footsteps hurried and rounded the corner.

I stepped out under the streetlight.

The two men who halted, startled, at the edge of the streetlight were big men wearing overcoats with their hats pulled low.

"Looking for someone, gentlemen?"

"Jeez!" one of them said.

His partner's hands went to his coat by habit. It was the goon I'd tangled with at Guido Manzetti's place. Around both men swirled the blacker-than-night mist of many dead, chained to them by circumstance and actions.

"You have something to say to me, Mickey?"

His face assumed a feral snarl and it was clear he had very little to say to me. His hands came out of his pocket with brass knuckles on both fists. His partner pulled a lead pipe from his coat and slapped it against his hand with enthusiasm.

"This is not going to end well, Mickey," I said. "Best to leave it here."

"You don't have Manzetti to protect you now, freak," Mickey said.

Not Born of Woman

"Neither do you," I pointed out.

"Get him, Joey," Mickey yelled.

Then there was no time for words as both of them came at me.

Joey swung the pipe at my left side as Mickey swung hard at my face with his brass knuckles.

I was able to slip Mickey's punch, but I blocked the pipe with my forearm so took a hard hit full on. I yelped involuntarily but shook it off to move between them, spinning just in time to block another right cross from Mickey.

I slapped an open hand into Mickey's chest to knock him back but that gave his confederate time to strike again, this time glancing a blow off my shoulder. It stunned me.

I staggered against a wall and Mickey followed his attack with a half dozen body shots to me with enough force to tell me he had ring experience. Joey could not swing his pipe while Mickey worked me over and he stood by, a fevered grin on his rough-hewn face.

"Get 'em, Mickey, bust him up!"

The thug took the encouragement from his crony and put even more force into his blows.

I was unable to block the punches as Mickey worked me like a heavy bag and I felt my ribs bruising from the punishment.

I'm not a skilled fighter, having relied so much on my strength in conflicts before and in my hunt for food in the arctic. I much disliked violence so had not made a study of it, but when my instincts for survival were aroused, they seemed to unleash a savage within me. It was something I actively resisted.

I managed to twist enough to get an elbow in to bear on Mickey's left temple. It was not a clean hit, but enough to knock him back. Unfortunately, this cleared the way for Joey to attack again.

The brute swung wildly at me but this time I was ready for him and managed to catch his right forearm with my left hand and grabbed his coat with my right. I jerked him with all my strength to launch him into the building behind me.

He slammed into the wall hard enough that I heard a snapping sound and he collapsed, limp, to the sidewalk.

"You son of a bitch," Mickey cursed. "We were just gonna cripple you, freak, but now I'm gonna gut you like a fish." He suddenly had a switchblade in his hand and lunged at me.

Before I realized it, I felt a pressure on my right thigh but quickly seized his knife arm and his coat collar and whirled him like a dance partner to slam him face first into the same wall as his comrade.

He slid to the ground unconscious, blood and broken teeth marking the facade of the building.

The violence ended, and I was abruptly aware of a long slash on my thigh where Mickey had cut me. It bled profusely though it did not sting yet.

Once I made sure the two of them still lived—which they did, though I suspected they would have to avail themselves of Saint Vincent's services and would be much inconvenienced for many days by their wounds. Mickey, for one, would remember me all his days when he looked into a mirror.

I stripped their wallets of all their cash, which I would drop in the poor box the next day and dropped the guns I found on them down the sewer grate.

At least I knew they wouldn't file a police report, so I'd have to tell Tommy I'd been a bad boy myself.

When I turned to walk home the pain of my bruised ribs pushed through my physical shock and my leg all but gave out under me. The wound was deep and more serious than I could handle on my own, so I knocked on Dottie's window.

Dottie was a nurse at Saint Vincent's Hospital who lived two doors down from me on the first floor. I'd met them on my first week in New York when they had been out sunning on their stoop. They had taken this stranger in a strange land under their wing and been a mother hen to help me with the awkward moments of a new arrival.

Fortunately, they were home and let me in right away.

Dottie, whose born name was Daniel, greeted me at their door in a dressing gown with full lipstick and make-up on, probably having just come in from a date. They affected women's clothes and favored men for companionship.

Not Born of Woman

I never understood how so many societies found that behavior unacceptable. I had seen it in the wild during my long isolation, as natural with all other species as with the human, the need for one being to find a sympathetic soul for companionship. Even I had come back to the clutter of mankind for the community.

"You did it this time, hunk," they gave their pet name for me as they looked at my leg wound. "But I have what we need here, I think. It's a long cut, but not too deep—I can stitch it up. Drop trousers!" I'd had occasion before to turn to Dottie for medical aid, though this was the most severe instance in the time I had known them.

Dottie did have the antiseptics, needles, and surgical thread necessary to sew up my wound. They dusted it with sulfur drugs against infection and bandaged it, forcing some cognac on me , they said, to deaden the pain, though it was not so great a discomfort I could not endure it.

"You were lucky it missed arteries and just skated across the surface," Dottie said as I eased my trousers back up and attempted to stand.

"Easy, hunk," they said. "Don't ruin my lovely stitch work, though in truth you have more than any quilt I've ever seen."

That made me smile. "You know I've lived an adventurous life, Dottie."

"And still do, dearie," they said. "You'd better baby that leg for a few days or you'll spout like a fountain."

"Thank you, D.,"

"My pleasure, hunk," they said. "I've been looking for any excuse to get you to drop trousers for years, eh?"

I laughed, but they continued, "Stop by in the morning so I can check that bandage and I think you'll need something for the pain."

"I'll be okay for that, but I'll stop by anyway."

I waved goodbye and hobbled next door, my leg smarting as I made my way slowly up the stairs to my lair, regretting I was on the third floor more with each step.

My pants were matted with blood, and I was so tired that I left them on as I stripped all else and fell into an immediate and dreamless sleep.

Teel James Glenn

I felt all my injuries with the dawn. The sun was shining brightly with the silvered cap on the Empire State building glowing like a wizard's wand.

My leg and my ribs both throbbed as I rolled out of my bed and limped to the window to look at the vista of the city.

I often felt alone in the vastness of those civilized canyons, connected and yet not connected to it all. There was still so much I did not understand about those beings out there. I felt that my destiny was here, not in the isolation that I had embraced for almost two hundred years, so I persisted.

Nietzsche said, "To live is to suffer, to survive is to find some meaning in the suffering." I had suffered and I searched for that meaning each day. Now I had a Romani girl and a priest who needed me, and their need gave me that day's meaning.

I showered and changed, careful not to disturb Dottie's bandage. I surrendered to the modern American penchant for pharmaceuticals and stopped down at Dottie's for some painkillers and a plate of eggs they insisted I have.

"Gotta keep those muscles fueled, big fella," Dottie said, always fussing over me. They were dressed in hospital scrubs and back to their Daniel persona. It pained me to think that D had to live in fear for their life choices in society as it was. I often worried for them.

"Thanks again, D," I said. "Still my mother hen!"

"Any time, hunk," they said. "But not too often, okay—I only have so much surgical thread."

I decided to rest my leg and called a cab to take me to the police station.

Tommy met me at the reception desk and led me into a small room with a stenographer.

"What happened to you?" Tommy asked as I settled into a chair. The laudanum that Dottie had given me helped but I had not done a very good job of hiding my limp.

Not Born of Woman

"Just me being clumsy," I lied. "Nothing of consequence."

"Okay, then," he said reverting to formal speech for the note taker's benefit. "If you would tell us the details of the incidents in your own words. Please state your full name, Mister Paradise."

I gave the name that was on my current forged papers, then recounted my visit to both Father Burton and all the events connected with the attempted murder. Tommy encouraged me to take a break afterward while some coffee was brought in.

"You never told me how Brendan's solo went," I asked as I sipped the coffee. It was barely drinkable, but it kept my mind off my leg.

"He was great," Tommy said with a proud father's enthusiasm. "Not the least bit nervous, like a real pro. He actually had two solos."

"Wonderful." I thought about the experience he had of seeing his child grow. It was perhaps the greatest joy of all living beings, in the lower forms and humans as well, to create life and watch it prosper. I had yet to meet his family, though I had seen pictures and heard many tales of their lives. I felt a real connection to them and that made me feel good to have roots of a sort after so long having none.

After a break I went through the full events of my visit to Otto Dorfman—only leaving out my client's name and the exact reason for my visit—as well as my actually entering the apartment, saying only I hoped to locate some family keepsakes.

Tommy prompted me with specific questions to clarify anything on which I was inexact, so in a little more than a half-hour the stenographer had recorded all I said. After we finished, a policewoman brought in the typed version of my statement about Father Burton.

Just as I signed that first statement an officer raced in.

"Detective Shane," the uniformed man said. "We got a match; the shot that killed the pawnbroker came from the same gun that was fired at the priest!"

My day was about to get very complicated.

CHAPTER EIGHT

Tommy and I were both stunned by that news.

"You sure there was no mistake?" Tommy asked the officer.

"We checked them twice in the lab, sir," the young officer said. "Both were fired from the same Mauser M1917 semi-automatic pistol. A 9mm Mauser Parabellum cartridge. There is no mistake."

"How is that possible?" I asked. Tommy looked at me.

"At this point, Adam, you are the only common denominator of the two I know of."

"But Dorfman was killed before you even told me about Father Burton's problem, Tommy. I didn't even know he existed as such at that point."

"I know," my friend said. "It doesn't make any sense to me either."

"At the moment," I said."I find that things make sense if you look at them from enough angles and long enough."

"Then let's go back to Father Burton's, Adam. We need to find out what this is really all about."

The trip was a fruitless one, for Father Burton still would not budge on his silence.

"I can not make the decision to violate the seal of the confessional," the priest said with obvious discomfort at the subject coming up again. "I have sent a request to my bishop but until I hear from him …."

"So, it is something you heard in the box," Tommy said.

"I cannot say."

The prelate's eyebrows knit in concentration and his internal struggle was written on his face, but his oath was stronger than any doubts he had. "I cannot confirm nor deny what you say." He shook his head. "I cannot comment further on this in any way. I am praying for guidance. Please leave me."

He physically turned away from us and I thought the priest was going to cry.

I looked to Tommy who, a man of deep faith himself, felt almost as bad for asking the priest as Burton did for denying us. That left it to me to say what had to be said.

"Father," I interjected, "you must understand that the man who shot at you killed a man the night before with the same gun and for all we know is still out there ready to kill someone else." I softened my tone to add a Thomas Aquinas quote, "'Every judgment of conscience, be it right or wrong, be it about things evil in themselves or morally indifferent, is obligatory, in such wise that he who acts against his conscience always sins.'"

He acknowledged my olive branch with a nod of his head, but it was clear he was done speaking, perhaps fearing he would let something slip inadvertently.

Tommy and I left, waving to the off-duty uniformed officer who was one of a dozen doing rotating shifts on their own time to protect the prelate.

"Stubborn," Tommy hissed in frustration when we were out of earshot of the recalcitrant prelate.

"Principled," I said. "Did not Jesus ask Peter to be his rock?"

"Don't blaspheme, Adam."

"No offense, Tommy," I said. He had no idea, of course, that if he knew my history, he would accuse me of being blasphemy incarnate. They had accused my creator of it and the events had spawned the family legend on which the Shelly woman based her fanciful novel. "But you have to admire this variety of stubbornness, my friend. His faith is strong."

"I know, Adam, but I feel helpless. If he would only let us help him."

"So, we work it from the other angle," I said. "Dorfman."

"I've already got some men tracing down all the recent customers," he said. "And we found a list of illicit acquisitions in his apartment. Not much doubt now that he was a fence."

I hadn't told Tommy that I had ventured into the apartment before he was called and already knew what was in that ledger.

"Can you tell me who your client is that required you to look to Dorfman?"

"I have principles as well," I said. "But I promise if it even remotely bears on this case, I will tell you."

He gave me a sidelong glance, but he knew I was as stubborn as Father Burton in my own way.

"Get out of here then," he finally said. "I have to earn my taxpayer paycheck."

"Talk to you tomorrow," I said.

I took a cab again to my office, the leg wound smarting considerably by now. Mort said there were no phone messages, so I assumed Vandoma and her brother were still going to keep their appointment. It was my hope that Nico could possibly provide some clue as to who might have known he had passed the *Koshti Bok* to the loan shark.

I had to assume that the killer was tracing the necklace. It was a guess—Dorfman could have been killed for any number of reasons, but I had no idea what they were and no real way of knowing. I would follow this thread until it worked out or proved pointless. It was something to do.

I took my time going up the stairs, regretting again my choice to be up long stairways. Maybe I would think about finding a building with an elevator if I moved.

I settled into my desk chair with a sigh so dramatic it made me laugh at myself. The pain, not as bad as I have ever had—it had been worse when a polar bear and I had a disagreement over a seal we both were hungry for. It took me many hours to crawl back to the icebound wreck and weeks of delirium before I was able to even think of hunting again. My creator endowed me with robust healing powers so I was confident my leg would recover in a short time. It would just hurt until then.

I took my journal out of my bottom drawer and occupied myself with updating entries—a habit I had gotten into over my long icebound time in the north. It both distracted and focused me.

At promptly two there was a knock on my outer door and Vandoma arrived, announcing herself and almost ritually asking permission to enter.

"Come in," I called. I closed the Encyclopedia Britannica I was reading—I was on to K again on this, my third reading of the set—and tried to look as non-threatening as possible. I almost forgot to put on my gloves and had just re-donned them as the Romani woman entered the outer office.

Today Vandoma wore a grey dress and the same blue jacket but had added a red silk scarf and small hat. She was also carrying a large handbag with a shoulder strap.

She was accompanied by a tall, dark man, carrying a heavy metal case, which I recognized as a typewriter. The man was clearly related to her with the same questing eyes, but with a certain suspicion in them as he glanced toward me. I felt he was assessing the cost of all the furnishing in the room with that look, as well.

He was dressed like a sharp with a bright brown double-breasted suit, a red wool scarf and a broad-brimmed yellow fedora with a red feather tucked in the band. He had a small pencil mustache, thick eyebrows, and a small gold hoop in his right ear.

"Mister Paradise," Vandoma said. "This is my brother, Nico Kalderash."

I chose to stand so Nico could get a better look at me. Dramatic, I admit, but sometimes it is easier than trying to impress with words.

"Pleased to meet you, Nico," I said. He looked at me with suspicion as he set the typewriter on the outer office's desk. Vandoma immediately unlatched the case as if she were ready to work.

"My sister has said you had some work for me," he said. He was direct, clearly a man who did not have time to waste.

I looked to the girl who removed a stack of papers from her bag and did indeed sit down at the outer desk to begin typing.

Smart girl.

"Yes," I said, "If you could come in here, I will tell you what I want."

Nico crossed the threshold into my inner office just as his sister set the typewriter keys to clicking, I suppose to give me some excuse to close the door though Nico only partly did so. He left the door slightly ajar, I had to assume, out of an excess of caution. This was not a man who trusted easily.

"What is this work you have for me?" He paused just inside the door when he realized there was little else in the room but the client chair, some bookshelves, and my desk. His eyes narrowed and he took a stance that implied he was ready to fight.

I sat down to attempt to defuse his anger. "You used your *Koshti Bok* to cover your gambling debts and things have gone bad because of it."

His suspicions were on full alert, so I pressed on. "Did you try to take it to Otto Dorfman first before you took it to Manzetti?" I saw him react to that and realized I had guessed right. "But he didn't offer enough, right? So, you went to the loan shark?"

He was across the room in an eye-blink and had a folding knife in his hand that he thrust menacingly at me.

I'd had enough of knives for the moment, so I reacted as well. I moved snake quick and grabbed his knife wrist, giving him just enough pressure to imply I could hurt him if I wanted to. "Stop this foolishness, Nico. I am here to help you recover the necklace."

I fixed him with my stare and saw his sudden realization that I could hurt him or more if I wanted to. There was a long moment when I saw he thought about trying to fight but then he relaxed, and I released his arm.

He stepped back and folded the knife and put it in his jacket again. That was good because if I had to leap up quickly from my chair, I was not sure at all my leg would have done the job.

"What do you want from me?" he asked.

Not Born of Woman

"Only the truth. I am not here to judge you or even comment on your gambling beyond the need to get the necklace back for your sister."

He looked to the door where the sound of typing was still steady. "So?"

"Answer my question honestly; did you visit Otto Dorfman the night before last when you heard he took it back from Guido?"

His eyes flickered and I suspect he considered lying but then said, "Yes; but when I got there the shop was closed and I didn't have a way to see him."

"You didn't go to his apartment upstairs, over the shop?"

"I didn't know he had one up there." He shrugged. "I didn't know what to do or how to find his home. So, I came back today but the shop was still closed."

"That's because Dorfman was killed yesterday."

"What?" His shock was real, but he recovered quickly. I saw the caged animal look come into his eyes.

"No one knows you were there," I said quickly. "You're not suspected of any crime, but I think the necklace may have something to do with it."

"I must leave the city."

"No, you must not," I said. "I told you you weren't connected to the death at the moment, but if they do discover the necklace was taken, they may look for you and if you leave it will proclaim guilt to everyone."

"Why should I listen to you?"

"Because I say you should," Vandoma was suddenly in the doorway.

"This is family business. Man's business," Nico hissed in Romani at her. "You had no business bringing this *gadjio* into this."

"You had no business using our *Koshti Bok* for your sickness. It is sacred."

"I am the man of the family; it is my right to do what I think is best. I would have gotten it back."

"How? By wishing it?"

"I have a sure thing at Belmont Park in—"

"No!" Vandoma came forward, sudden fury in her eyes. She seemed abruptly taller than her sibling and for a moment I thought she was going to strike him but instead she snatched up the edges of her skirt and slapped him at his waist with it.

I saw him go white with shock and gasp. He actually jumped away from her as if he had been stung by a scorpion.

"Sister!" He murmured, sounding broken.

"Go," she said. "Get cleansed and reflect on what you have done to the honor of the family Kalderash!"

He made a sound like a sob and raced out of the room.

CHAPTER NINE

Only after he had left the office did she suddenly seem to realize I had witnessed the entire scene. She turned to me, the fire in her eyes fading, and lowered her gaze as if ashamed.

"Forgive me, Mister Paradise," she whispered meekly in English. "That was the shame of—"

"You forget I know the *Romano*," I said to her in Romani. The Romano was the complex set of rules that govern things such as cleanliness, purity, respect, honor, and justice in their world. "I know that *Rromano* means to behave with dignity and respect as a Roma person, Miss Kalderash. And I know that to strike a man with the skirts of a woman is to mark him as unclean and he must rush to perform certain ceremonies to be pure again."

The strict rules with the traveling, tribal peoples such as the Roma had come about to preserve order in their camps and were deeply ingrained. One of the strictest was the preservation of the purity of the women and to do so any part of her below the waist was considered 'unclean' to any but her husband. To be touched by a woman's skirts meant that a man must immediately take steps, or he would be banished from the tribe.

"You—you really do know the *Romanipen*," she said with a little awe in her voice. It was the philosophy of her people of which the *Rromano* were the codified rules.

"Yes," I said, reverting to English. "And you were very clever to force him to head home with that act; it saved a lot of arguing." This brought a shy smile from her, as I complimented her.

"I must know what is happening," she said. Her earnestness was sobering.

"Fair enough," I replied. "Please sit." She took the client's chair, and I told her what I had discovered so far—or rather that I had not discovered. It was easy to talk to her.

She listened without comment, her gaze steady and intense, absorbing and analyzing all I said.

When I was done, she said, "My brother did not hurt this pawn store man, this I know."

"How?"

"If my brother wished to kill, he would not use a gun, he would use a knife and it would be face-to-face. He is hot of blood but not that kind of evil."

"I agree with you," I said. "He is also not the type to torture. I believe, after seeing him that is certain, but you must understand I needed to know so I may continue with no doubts."

"What will you do now?" Her tone was disappointed because she sensed that I really was at a dead end with no direction to pursue.

"I honestly do not know," I admitted. "But don't give up hope. I'll work another angle; I just have to think."

She took this in for a moment and nodded.

"I, too, will think," she said. She rose and went into the outer office where her typewriter was set up and sat at the desk. "I will work on the manuscript I brought while I do."

I stood and limped over to the doorway; she noticed my odd walk.

"What has happened to you?"

"Oh, just a little mishap," I said. "Nothing; it will be okay in a day or so."

Her brow furrowed. "You do not speak truth." That made me grin.

"Really," I said. "I've had worse."

"This happened because of what I asked of you, is it not so?"

I could not lie to her. "Indirectly; but really it is okay."

"I do not want others to suffer for my brother's weakness." A cloud passed over her features and I found I didn't like it.

"Understand, Miss Kalderash, that I do not suffer. Aren't the pillars of the *Rromani* Code of *baxt* that is honor and *ladž*, shame? And there is no shame in honorable action. What you have asked of me is honorable, by returning the *Koshti Bok* to prevent the shame of your family from being revealed."

"*You do* understand the Roma way," she said again with slight awe. "This is not common."

"I have been told I am not common, it is true," I said. "I think in the Romani world you are not either." I meant it as a compliment, but I saw her manner darken again.

"It is why I have not been promised," she said, and a subtle head gesture indicated her hunchback. "None want to continue the curse."

"The body is not the container of curses, Vandoma," I said, risking familiarity. "Only the housing for possibilities. It is the soul that may carry remnants of bad decisions from—maybe another life?"

"You know what it is to be looked on as different," she said with unusual directness. "This is perhaps why you understand the Romani way—we who have always been outside the *gadjo* world."

"'My heart is ten times lighter than my looks,'" I quoted from *Richard III*. "I think all are outsiders who let themselves be."

We looked at one another for a long moment, both hanging at the edge of words but neither sure what was safe to say. I chose a common point for all living things—hunger.

"Would you care for some food?" I asked, "I can get some sandwiches from the store below."

She seemed relieved by the distraction. "Yes," she said. "But I will go down for them, Mister Paradise—you should not have to go down the stairs."

"Okay," I said, "I'll write a note so Jake will put it on my tab. And some soda pop as well." I stepped to the desk, and she handed me a sheet of typing paper where I wrote out a note for the boy at the counter and added a note for some aspirin as my leg was throbbing.

"I shall not be long," she said with a cheery smile, glad, I suppose for the reason to leave my looming presence and the unspoken things between us.

The clicking of her heels on the stairs was oddly comforting as I limped back to my desk and sat again.

In my time in New York, indeed in my time in Sweden and then Paris before I chose to come to the Empire City, I had made many acquaintances, had worked hard to be among others and found many other outsiders but there was something different about the *Romani* woman. Did she see beyond my flesh mask to the searching being within? It was the very thing that compelled me to assume the profession of investigator—with no story of my own I looked to find a story. Why her story should speak to me so much was confusing to me.

"Woolgathering, Adam?" Tommy Shane was standing in the outer doorway and walked in with light steps. He went to the client chair and sat.

"I guess so," I said. "But you do have a burglar's tread." This made him laugh.

"Maybe my career in another life," he said trying to look mysterious.

"What made you venture up the long flight?"

"News," he said. "I didn't want to wait for you to come out of your lair."

"And?"

"We discovered that Dorfman was running a little side business—"

"Besides being a fence?"

"Actually, yes. It appears he was deliberately looking for religious objects from various faiths, actively hunting them down. And he seems to have been dealing with the swastika boys."

I knew this, already, of course, so it was not a surprise to me, but I had to pretend it was.

"Wow," I said, "they're getting to be a nuisance in the city."

"That's an understatement," he snorted. "They seem to be really trying to keep in the spotlight since their rally. A lot of bullying incidents. With these missing girls' cases at the same time, the department is strapped for overtime."

"So where does this lead us?"

"I want to go and canvas the pawnshops to see if anyone else is doing the same thing—it's possible they decided to horn in on Dorfman's business."

Not Born of Woman

"Makes sense."

"But—"

"But you don't have the manpower and you'd like me to go?"

"You are bright despite what Sergeant Morris says."

I laughed at his remark. "Okay," I said. "I'll get on it tomorrow; I'm a bit slow today."

"Leg still bothering you?"

"It'll pass."

"Here is a list of the shops we think are even slightly shady." He pulled a sheet of typescript from his coat. "This will make it a little easier."

"You are too kind." I took it and looked it over, with a fair number of shops in the Bronx as well as the group on Eighth Avenue.

At that moment Vandoma returned with our food. She brought a Pastrami sandwich with everything for me and set it and my Dixi-Cola on the edge of the desk. She gave a contained smile to Tommy and then retreated to the outer office to her typewriter without giving me a chance to introduce her to Tommy.

My friend watched her go, then looked back at me with a curious expression. "Upgrading? Business improving that much you can afford a secretary?"

It was a little too complicated to explain so I just shrugged. "Evolution," I said.

Tommy stood up. "Well, I'll let you eat and head back; they think they found one of those missing girls down by South Street; a floater."

"There's been more noise on those deaths than usual with such cases," I said. There'd been a number of high-profile missing person cases of young girls in the last two weeks.

"*The Daily Star* played it up big because one of them was a relative of the newsroom head," Tommy said. "But it would have caught our attention eventually—too many similarities with the girls—teen, redheads or blondes, not problem kids. I just hope we can find the others before it's too late."

"A series criminal?"

"Seems like it. I'll check in when I can," he said as he went out through the outer office, tipping his hat to Vandoma. "Ma'am."

When he closed the outer door, I called out.

"You can come in now, Vandoma," I said. "The scary policeman is gone. Bring in your lunch."

The *Roma* woman came in carrying her sandwich and a soda and sat in the client chair.

"I do not like *baulo*," she said in explanation using vulgar slang for police. "Always they say, 'Gypsies are criminals, Gypsies are thieves, Gypsies are dirty ….' We Roma are *not* such things."

I was a bit surprised by the vehemence of her reaction to Tommy, though I should not have been. "You knew he was a cop just by looking?"

She nodded. "I could feel it."

"So, you do have the sight?"

She looked at me with a wary expression, unsure if I was making fun of her, but when she realized I was not said, "My mother does, she is a *chovihanis*, a healer, and a *drukker*—she who sees the future. They say I do not because of my affliction, but I can read the cards and the lines in one's hand."

I had touched a sore spot again and so I let it lie while we both ate in silence. There was a quiet dignity to her that I had not found in many in my time among civilization.

After a time, she asked, "You eat such things often?"

"Yes," I said. "I don't cook much, as I only have a hotplate in my apartment, which is why your home-cooked meal will be so welcome to me."

"You have a new way to look for the *Koshti Bok*?"

"Possibly." I told her about the pawnshop list that Tommy had brought me and how I planned to canvas them. She shook her head.

"No," she said with finality. "Your leg is not so good, and you could not go to so many in a day."

"Really?" I smiled. "Then how do you suggest I search for brokers looking to buy religious articles?"

"I will tell my tribe to look for these things," she said. "Not of the *Koshti Bok*, of course, but that you are looking for such objects."

"You can do that?"

Not Born of Woman

"My family has status," she pointed out with obvious pride. "And my brother will not speak of his shame in telling the others when I tell them to look for these things." She cleaned off my desk and took the list Tommy had given to me. "I will type some copies of this."

She didn't wait for permission but went out to the desk she had claimed as her own and slipped in paper and carbon to begin making copies.

CHAPTER TEN

I sat at my desk a little bit amazed by the Roma woman's sudden take-charge attitude. I found myself with nothing to do but consider my next move as well as try to find all the connections between Nico's actions and the death of the pawnbroker.

My first job was to keep the Roma's involvement in the case from Tommy and the police as long as possible, but that would get harder if they found out I was using a network of Romani looking for the bauble.

While I pondered my next course of action the outer door opened, and a young Negro boy entered. "Excuse me, Ma'am," the boy said to Vandoma, "is Mister Paradise in?"

"I will see," she said, acting the part of a secretary. She started to rise from her desk, but I stepped to the door.

"It's okay, Vandoma," I called. "I'm called Adam Paradise, son."

He stared up at me with wide eyes. "Wow, you're tall!"

"I suppose I am," I laughed. "What can I do for you?"

"Mister Digger Tome sent this over for you, sir," the boy said. He held up a brown paper-wrapped package. I took it and fished a silver dollar out of my pocket for him.

"Holy Moley," he said. "A dollar! Gee thanks, mister!"

"Tell Digger thanks for me," I said as I opened the wrapping.

It was a book with a note from my friend. "This may help you in your search, Adam. I'd forgotten I had it in the back. Digger."

"Forgot," I said out loud. "You didn't forget—I'll bet you went out and bought it to send to me."

"What is it?" the Roma woman asked. I held it up.

Not Born of Woman

"It is a book called *"Amuletae boni et mali*—Amulets of Power; Evil and Good," I said. "Written in the seventeen hundreds in Latin, with some notations in Hebrew here in the margins."

"You can read this?" she said with a bit of awe.

"Yes, The Latin easily, but my Hebrew is less exact; something I should work on correcting," I answered as I leafed through the leather-bound volume. There were a number of engravings within, of various religious objects. "This is a Vatican document dealing with summoning occult power." I paged through it with her looking over my shoulder. "For a religion that often decries such sorcerous things, they are known to have many of them in their private collection."

"There!" she cried as she pointed to an illustration of a necklace. "That is the *Koshti Bok!*"

"Yes," I said. "The text says it is a famous necklace and talisman of the Kalderash Clan of the Romani."

"It truly is a thing of great power," she whispered. "The tales of my family—"

"I understand, Vandoma; while you know a myth to be true in your heart it is still a different thing to have it confirmed. Believe me, I know of such things—myth and reality, that is."

She looked at me oddly but simply said, "There is much, Mister Paradise, that you understand, this I know now. I think it is not a *booja*—a trick of the universe that led me to contact you."

"I will read this in-depth now," I said. "And I will tell you what I find."

"I will make the lists and then type the work I brought with me for the adventure magazines."

And that is what we did for the next few hours, with her typing steadily while I explored the arcane text. The sound of the keys and the ringing of the bell at the end of each line were oddly comforting while I read of some objects from across Europe, India, and Asia that the Roman Church decided had powers that could be harnessed for their use or should be kept from others they determined were evil.

Whether real or not, such beliefs had moved many to action of mankind—dark actions—for many years. And now it seemed that a new generation of adepts and would-be adepts looking to seize power for themselves were using things like the *Koshti Bok* of the Romani.

I was suddenly conscious that the typing had stopped and became aware that the woman was looking at me as I read. When she saw me look up, she spoke.

"I have done all I brought with me," she said. "I should go home and bring this list to my brother so that he may bring it to our tribe."

I told her what I'd read in the book, so far. Again, I was struck by how intently she listened and how much of what I said she grasped.

"So, this is a book of the Roman Church on things that can be used for evil and which must be destroyed?" The darkness of what she said weighed heavily on her.

"Not exactly," I said with a short laugh. "It enumerates objects of power that the Roman Church feared could be used to rival their own power. What they could not control, the leaders in Rome feared and thus destroyed. Like the Mayan alphabet, or the Druids of Britannia."

"And my own people's beliefs," she finished.

"Yes," I said. "And it seems someone else is attempting to gather such objects for their own purposes. Perhaps the National Socialists in Europe and here, from what I have heard."

She looked at the book as if it were a creature that would bite her, then up at me. "Is there really hope to recover the *Koshti Bok*?" There was so much pain in her voice I reached out a gloved hand to touch her wrist.

"There's always hope, Miss Kalderash; isn't the spirit of the Romani undiminished by centuries of suspicion and hate from the outside? It is hope for a better world of your own self-determination. Let that hope live here in this time; with your help, we will find your necklace."

She patted my hand with her other and said, "Thank you, Mister Paradise. I think you are a good man ... but—" To my surprise, she took the edge of my glove and began to slip it off.

"What?"

"I have not the sight of my mother, but I can see in the lines of your hand that which is to be."

Not Born of Woman

For some reason, I found myself unable to stop her as she slid the glove off of me and then turned my hand over for her to do her chiromancy.

"I can read that which was in the lines and mounds as well," she said in a serious voice. "Perhaps I can learn about you, Mister Paradise."

"You may not want to learn some things about me, Miss Kalderash."

"Is not knowledge power?" She stared hard at my left hand. "But I must look at both of your hands, for in your left hand is your natural talent, personality, and what you've been through so far, while right hand tells of your future. The left is what God gives you, the right is how you make use of it."

She reached for my other gloved hand, but I resisted. "I do not think you want to look at my past, miss. And I have no real desire to look at my future."

"I must see who you are, Adam Paradise." She spoke softly but firmly. "I came to you to help in recovering the *Koshti Bok*, but now lives are involved, and my tribe will be drawn in. I do not see as my mother does, so I must know."

"As you will," I said and slid off my right glove. She looked at the two different hands with a little intake of breath. My left was paler and square fingered, my right darker and with long, thinner fingers.

She considered them both for a moment, clearly trying not to show her surprise but it was there. Surprise, but no fear; that was something new to me.

"This 'M' line on your left hand means you are blessed, Mister Paradise," she said with awe. "See here—the heart line, lifeline, headline, and fate line all connect to make it." She looked up at me and her expression softened. "It's also a sign of strong intuition and creativity. It shows great determination."

"I try," I said. In my long life, I had not had such a circumstance as the palm reading and had no truck with it. A gap in my education. "My life has a different shape than most."

Why am I permitting this? How is it that I open myself to this woman?

"And this curve," she continued, "runs alongside the lifeline—it is a guardian angel line. The line where it cuts your headline says at what age they passed." She stared at it for a long time then up at me. "But—this can not be right? Your lifeline—there are several beside each other. I have never seen this."

I could only smile. "Perhaps it is best to let it be, Vandoma. Know that I wish to help you and do all I can to get back your family's good luck."

She stood across from me, holding my hands, obviously conflicted to look at my right hand but then looked up into my eyes. "As you wish, Mister Paradise. I have faith." She let my hands go and went to the outer office to pack her things.

I re-donned my gloves, reached into my desk drawer, and walked out to her. "These are a spare set of keys to the door downstairs and the office, Miss Kalderash. Why not leave your typewriter and come back tomorrow to do more of your work? And you can make this the center for your tribe to contact you with what they find."

She looked up at me, still obviously a little stunned by what she had seen or guessed in my hand. "Yes, this is a good idea." She took the keys, picked up her bag and put her typed manuscript in it.

"Let's walk down together," I said. "I've had a full day and I still have one stop to make on the way home."

She was patient and quiet as I locked the outer door and limped down the steps. At the bottom, she nodded goodbye and walked off into the crowd, the ghostly shapes of ancestors floating around her.

For some reason, I felt afraid I might not see her again, and that thought bothered me.

I was hungry again, so I said goodnight to Mort and Jake and walked back downtown to a small diner I often ate at on Fourteenth and Sixth Avenue. I ate a full meal—I guess my body was using up a lot of energy healing my leg—but afterward decided I didn't want to go directly back to my studio.

My head was swimming with the events of the day, so I thought a little distraction was in order. The choice for such was to go to the Variety Photoplay Movie Theater on Third Avenue off Fourteenth Street. It was a small theatre that had been a Vaudeville theater in the past where performers like the Great Houdini had appeared.

I had timed it just right to catch the newsreel and stopped at the concession stand in the tiny lobby, then went to wedge myself into a seat at the back of the house with some popcorn (one of the things I had come to treasure about American culture) and some soda pop. I settled in to enjoy my anonymity for a while.

The news of the day did little to lighten my mood, with footage of that Austrian fellow Hitler giving a speech before the Reichstag that talked about naval expansion programs and Neville Chamberlain warning that any German attack on France would bring an attack by Britain in retaliation.

Even the audience in the darkened room, only about half what most Thursday nights would normally be owing to the cold and rain, collectively sighed at the gloomy news.

It did not help the atmosphere in the room when the next item was about last week's American Bund Rally at Madison Square Garden. Footage came on screen of the seventeen hundred uniformed police officers patrolling outside the venue with thirty-five firefighters, armed with a heavy-duty fire hose in preparation for the riot that everyone expected. Tommy had told me about how bomb squads combed the arena in response to threats received the week before. The threats had boasted of a series of time-activated devices to explode during the event. Fortunately, they had been empty threats.

Most of the theater audience cheered when the footage was shown of protestors around Madison Square Garden carrying signs stating, "Smash Anti-Semitism" and "Drive the Nazis Out of New York."

The newsreel gave way to a trailer for some new films, a short on duck hunting, and then the first chapter of a Republic Serial, *The Lone Ranger Rides Again*. It was a fun bit of triviality with a masked hero that left him in danger at the end.

Teel James Glenn

    A new film called *Stagecoach* was next and I must say I enjoyed it, if only for its morality play aspect and plea for acceptance of each person on their own merits. I also thought that perhaps, someday, I would enjoy learning to ride a horse. When I had last been among mankind, I had had no opportunity to do so.

    For the three hours of my time in the darkened theater, I was able to let my mind wander and once more enjoyed seeing the world as I imagined mankind did, albeit in black and white. On the screen was a world without ghosts floating around and I imagined it was how most people saw the world.

    It was good to lose myself in the fantasy and I felt refreshed as I walked across Thirteenth Street near midnight. Dottie's lights were off so I decided my leg wound, which was feeling considerably better, would not suffer from having the bandage on it another night. I would see if they were around in the morning to check it, but I was pretty sure I would be able to dispense with a bandage in the next day or so.

    I was feeling relaxed and ready to get a good night's sleep when I opened the door to my studio and had the gun shoved in my face.

CHAPTER ELEVEN

"Don't bother to get comfortable, Paradise," a shadowed figure said from behind that gun. "We will be leaving presently."

A second gunman met us as the first escorted me out the door of my apartment. The pair bracketed me as we walked down the stairs. A late-model sedan waited out front and I was escorted into the back with my two new friends on either side, guns pressed into my ribs.

I noted that one of the guns was a Mauser.

"And to what do I owe this visit, gentlemen?"

"Shut up, freak," the blond to my right said. He was a man who appeared in his twenties, lean and athletic. His companion was built in a similar mold, though broader. A third Nordic type was driving.

"Are we going to a Bund rally?" I asked.

"I said, shut up." He poked me with his pistol. "You'll talk when we ask you to and not before."

Dark shapes swirled around these men, murky grey and deep indigo phantoms of the dead that were chained to these fanatics by past violence. Despite their comical tough guy attitudes and self-important manner, they were actually dangerous and had certainly taken lives.

The car drove through the quiet night streets for a while, going down through Chinatown and across the Brooklyn Bridge into that borough and along Flatbush Avenue. We sat in not very companionable silence. My two back seat comrades kept eyes on me, their weapons jammed uncomfortably into my sides.

I suppose I could have tried to resist, though both of my abductors stayed vigilant enough that to do so would certainly result in my being shot. The best course of action seemed to be inaction, waiting to learn what it was they wanted.

In time we pulled up in front of a warehouse way out in Coney Island, not far from the amusement area and beach. The smell of the salt air was a sharp change from the city smell of Manhattan and would have been refreshing but for the circumstances of my arrival in Brooklyn.

"No funny moves, big guy," the abductor who had first spoken said. He seemed to be in charge and exited the car in a narrow alley where we were hidden from the street. He was very professional in backing away, keeping the gun trained on me. "In that door."

A fourth individual met us at the door and carefully backed away from us, also with a drawn gun in hand.

I must have a pretty scary reputation, or they are incredibly insecure! Or Both.

I was herded to a stairwell and down into a damp basement where aisles of boxes were stored. We moved in stony silence with all three pistols trained on me to potentially deadly effect.

"Sit," the blond leader ordered when we reached a lone chair set in the center of a cleared space among a canyon of boxes. It was a metal office chair on wheels with handcuffs already attached to the arms. Apparently, I was not in for a pleasant time.

I sat and the man who'd met us zoomed in and snapped the cuffs on my arms.

"Secure?" the leader asked.

"Yes, Hans," the local said. This statement seemed to lift a weight from my captor's shoulders and then all holstered their guns.

"Now, Mister Paradise," Hans said. "Why did you steal from Otto Dorfman? And where are the objects you took?"

It occurred to me that I was going to be in for a very long night.

"I don't think you really understand what is going on, Hans," I said. This did not please him and he darted in and slapped my face.

"I will not have any of your mongrel lies," he said.

He was not far wrong with my pedigree, strictly speaking, but I didn't think he was splitting hairs here. His was a very narrow view of genetics and I am sure he had no category for me.

"I will not lie to you," I said flatly. "I have no reason to."

"Good," he said. "That will save you some pain."

"I would hope so."

"Tell me what you did with what you took from Dorfman."

"And that is where our realities diverge," I said. "I took nothing."

He slapped me again. This time, harder. His smile was savage, almost demonic.

"Swine!" he said, a slight accent coming through his English now. "You were seen at his apartment after he had been murdered. You talked to the police to cover your theft."

"You are incorrect," I said. "Hitting me will not change the facts. I found the pawn dealer tortured and dead when I arrived at his apartment. Frankly, I thought you had done it."

This statement did not please Hans and he laid into me with a series of blows, varying his technique from slaps to my face to punches to my body. I have a fairly high pain threshold, or so I calculate from my knowledge of most people, but it still hurt, particularly my already beleaguered ribs.

After he exhausted himself, he stepped back.

I looked at him. "Physically assaulting me will not change the reality. I did not kill nor steal from Mister Dorfman."

"Your stubbornness and lies don't fool us," Hans said. "But we have time. Perhaps if you contemplate your fate for a time, you will tell us the truth." He waved for the others, and they rolled my chair to the edge of an open pit-like shaft in one corner of the basement. Dark phantom shapes hovered over it, and I knew that others had died in that place.

The Bundists attached a rope to the back of the chair.

"You'll have some time to consider that your life is in our hands, Mister Paradise," Hans said. "Speak only the truth when we pull you up or it will be a short life."

I took delight in the fact that the four men grunted considerably as they lowered me over the edge of the pit and slowly let me down some twenty feet to the bottom of the eight-foot square space.

"Think, Paradise," Hans said. "And reflect on your mortality in the darkness."

The chair bumped to the bottom with a jar and then the rope coils were dropped to the floor beside me. I heard the four Bundists laughing as they left the basement, and the lights went out so that I was in sudden and intense, pitch darkness. There was the smell of death in that place, not recent, but very real.

It was not the first time I had been in a dark damp place that echoed the grave, but it was the first time I had been so confined intentionally.

After a few moments, I heard the scuttering sounds of rats in the corners of the pit and from above me in the basement.

At least I have company.

I set about freeing myself first as a prelude to escape. The cuffs were standard police-type cuffs and had been intentionally clamped painfully tight on my wrists. I concentrated for a few moments then jerked hard on them both with all my might. The links holding both cuffs to the ones attached to the chair arms snapped, though not without pain. This made the single cuffs I wore dig deeper into my wrists. I am sure I felt blood.

I would have to deal with the newly acquired jewelry when I could get a lock pick from my pocket and had some time. My immediate issue was finding a way out of the concrete pit. I felt my way around and determined that there was a drain in the floor, which was probably related to a sump of some sort. The metal grate on the floor was barely a hands-width wide, so there was no outlet there for my size.

I walked the perimeter of the space and confirmed it was a square of rough concrete, but not so rough I could find a purchase for finger holds to climb out.

I considered what would happen next. The blond abductors would undoubtedly leave me in the dark, damp pit for some considerable length of time hoping to break my spirit and then resume their interrogation, presumably with greater intensity—though how, or if they even planned to extract me from the pit was a mystery to me. I suspected they would question me and then kill me to join the other dead things in the pit for the rats to feast on.

So, it made sense I should not be in the pit when they returned.

And speaking of mystery, if they did not assault and kill the pawnbroker who had been acquiring the magical objects for them,

Not Born of Woman

then—who did? There was someone, or more than one individual, new in the equation and that meant that going forward I had to be even more alert.

I lay face down on the floor of the space with my feet firmly against one wall and my arms extended, so my palms were on the opposite wall. As I am a little over seven feet tall this gave me some play in my arms. By pressing upward, which is to say ahead of me, I was able to wedge myself upward, an inch at a time.

As Cervantes said, "Truth will rise above falsehood as oil above water." So it was that I worked myself up the shaft, muscles straining. It was painfully slow, and my thigh wound was on fire, but once I began, I had no choice but to keep at it.

Time dilated and folded inward on itself so that there was no yesterday or tomorrow, only the constant *now* of pressing on. My muscles locked and strained but I kept my mind blanked to that and concentrated on keeping tension in my limbs. I rose, inch by torturous inch, until my fingers felt the edge of the pit.

Here was the tricky part of my ascent, to make the transition from my extended body position to get over the lip of the pit. The moment I got my fingers over the top, only the heels of my hands keeping the pressure up, I straightened my arms to bend my knees a bit then launched myself forward to grab the edge with my fingertips.

My body swung down and slammed painfully into the wall, but I had prepared for the jarring collision and was able to hold on with just my fingertips. After catching my breath, I levered myself up and rolled onto my back on the floor of the basement where I lay breathing hard and letting my cramped limbs rest.

After some time, I regained my faculties and rose gingerly to my feet.

My wrists were painful from the cuffs, my forearms slick with blood, so I paused for several minutes to use the lockpick in my pocket to remove them. It was a welcome relief when I removed the second one and I relished the sting of freedom, however minor when they were off.

The room was still in pitch darkness, so I had to grope my way carefully along, working to remember the layout from before my descent into my personal Inferno. "Where we came forth, and once more saw the stars." Dante Alighieri's last words from that work came to mind as I felt my way around a stack of crates and saw a sliver of light from beneath the doorway to the stairs.

Now was the time for caution, because there was a good chance my kidnappers would be upstairs. I was stiff from my climb but was able to move relatively quietly, taking care to put my weight on the outside of the wooden runners to limit the creaking.

At the top of the stairs was a second door and there was a light on the other side of it.

I stopped and listened.

"If you've finished all the pamphlets we can head out." I recognized Hans's voice.

One of the men who had taken me said, "How long?"

"I want a hot meal and a couple hours of sleep," the leader said. "So just lock up and we can come back in the morning. The longer that freak sits in the cold and dark the less work we'll have to get the truth out of him."

"What if he was telling the truth?" a third voice said.

"It doesn't matter," Hans said with obvious delight in his tone. "When we are sure he can tell us no more we finish him and fill in the pit. It's time anyway, it was starting to stink." There was laughter at that, followed by the sound of the lock on the other side of the door turning, then footsteps, the light going off, and another door opening and closing.

I listened for a time until I was certain that I was alone in the building then I applied my shoulder to the door and burst the lock.

I found myself in an office off to one side of the warehouse with some ambient light coming in from high-up windows. There were several cardboard boxes near some desks, and I took a chance to turn on one of the desk lamps and opened a box.

"The German American Federation is all American," was in red letters across the front of the pamphlet I removed from the box. "Remember George Washington was the first Fascist—he knew that Americans needed a strong hand to guide them."

Not Born of Woman

The delusion of the Bundists was astounding even to me who often found civilizations' artificialities and the rationalizations of extreme groups absurd. While I patted my bloody wrists where the cuffs had chaffed me with a handkerchief from my jacket pocket, I read the offal of their credo.

The pamphlet went on to list the ranks of the stormtroopers, called the *Ordnungs-Dienst* (OD), or "Orderly Service," and touted that they were trained in marching, rifle shooting, and self-defense, among other things. It claimed they were present at all Bund events and rallies with instructions to ensure the safety of Bund members. They then went on to equivocate that the OD was not a military body, and OD members were not permitted to carry weapons other than police batons. Yet it was clear that their similarities to the dangerous Nazi storm troopers in Germany were very much paramilitary. There were also quotes from their American *Führer*, Fritz Kuhn, that were passionately pro-Nazi and antisemitic.

Such a lovely group of people I have as enemies. As Oscar Wilde said, "A man cannot be too careful in the choice of his enemies."

I seemed to have chosen well.

CHAPTER TWELVE

I was forced to walk a good distance along Surf Avenue in Brooklyn's Coney Island, grateful for the fresh sea air after my time in the death pit, before I came to the elevated train platform. There I waited considerably longer before a late-night train took me back into Manhattan.

I was sore, tired, and a bit angry by the time I returned home with the throb of my leg wound the least of my aches.

I took a hot shower, put some salve Dottie had given me on my chaffed wrists and then fell into bed for a few hours' sleep. I was fairly certain the Bundists would not even know I had escaped until the morning, but I piled furniture against my door to be sure I got my rest, uninterrupted.

Five hours later I awoke refreshed though still a bit sore. My leg wound was almost healed, a testament to the recuperative powers with which my creator had gifted me. I dressed and carefully exited my apartment, keenly aware of my surroundings and alert for any ambush.

I once more opted for a taxicab up to the office and went into Mort's drug store for breakfast and some conversation.

"Hi, Mister P," Jake said as I sat down on the stool at the counter. The freckle-faced boy was always a cheerful bright spot in the city. He had another Bobbysoxer at the counter as well, different from the one the other day, stopping by on her way to high school to flirt for a bit.

"Morning, Jake," I said. "A bacon and egg sandwich and a coffee to go, please."

Not Born of Woman

The young man set about making it while still chatting with the girl, who giggled, "So I'll see you later, Jake." She smiled and waved, blushing when he saluted with a spatula, barely noticing me with stars in her eyes for the young man.

"I'm amazed you get any work done here," I said to him when he served me my coffee cup and the sandwich wrapped in brown paper . He grinned.

"Gotta keep myself busy, Mister P," he said.

"If you paid as much attention to your work around here, young man," Mort said, coming from the back, behind his pharmacy counter, "I would be a millionaire!" The old man hid his grin.

"Aw, come on, guys," the red-haired Jake said. "I'm just a regular fella."

"A regular Clark Gable," Mort said with a good-natured jibe.

"More like Andy Hardy," I offered, and they both laughed.

"How are you today, Adam?" the proprietor asked me.

"A little more tired than usual, Mort," I admitted.

"Your leg looks better," Mort said. "No limp."

"Yes, it is better today," I admitted. "But I did want to talk to you about, well, possibly getting some tutoring from you."

"Tutoring, Adam, in what?"

"Hebrew," I said. His look was not quite startled, but not far from it. "I have a rudimentary knowledge but would like to learn more."

"He's a great tutor, Mister P," Jake offered. "He's helping me get ready for my college entrance exams."

"Thanks, Jake," The white-haired man laughed again then gave me a wide smile. "*Fraynd*, for a Gentile you are a pretty good Jew."

"I take that as a great compliment, my friend. But I am serious."

"Of course, I would love to help you learn more," he said. "Stop down later and we will have your first lesson."

"Please tell me how I can compensate you for your time," I said.

"Oh no, my friend," he said. "I cannot take money for such a *mitzvah*."

"Did not Nachman of Bratslav say, 'Knowledge that is paid for will be longer remembered?'" This made my friend laugh with delight.

"You are a regular *mensch*!" he said. "We will discuss it later, my well-read friend."

I thanked him and waved to Jake then went up the stairs to my office. As I walked down the hall, the sound of typing came to my ears. It made me oddly happy to hear.

"Good morning, Miss Kalderash," I said as I walked into the outer office. Vandoma was seated at the desk working diligently on a manuscript.

"Good morning, Mister Paradise."

She was wearing a dark green dress today with her hair held back with a green ribbon. Her smile was guarded, and I suddenly remembered her reaction to reading my palms the day before and felt it might have offended or frightened her. And that disturbed me. I did not want to frighten her.

"I did not realize you would be up here so soon, or I would have brought you a coffee," I said.

"That's fine," she said without looking up from her typing. "I had some before I came in."

"How are you doing today?" I asked.

She stopped and looked up with a neutral expression. "Fine. Should I not be?"

"Uh ... what are you typing?"

She sighed and held up a pulp magazine like the ones in the racks below. It was an issue of *The Void* with a lurid painting of the black-masked figure looming over a scantily clad woman who was tied to a train track. Then she nodded to the manuscript on the right. "The writer of this is a terrible speller, so I must read it as I type to correct spellings when I can. There is much shooting." She said the last with an annoyed tone.

"My sympathies."

"My brother has taken the list of the things you gave me to the members of the tribe." She said this as if needing to change the subject, or perhaps reminding me this was a work relationship. "Some will come in today when they know things."

"Excellent." I walked past her to set my coffee and sandwich on my desk. I hung up my coat and hat, then sat down to enjoy my meal. I

Not Born of Woman

noticed that the book I'd received yesterday from Digger was not on the corner of the desk where I thought I'd left it.

I unwrapped my sandwich and looked around for the book, thinking perhaps I had moved it last evening. I had, after all, not really gotten the rest I needed.

While I wandered around the office eating, I happened to glance out the window to Fifth Avenue. I noticed that a familiar dark-haired figure was coming into Mort's store, accompanied by two others.

Not what I need this morning.

I put down the remainder of my food, took a quick sip of my coffee and stepped into the outer office.

"I have to go downstairs for a moment," I said to Vandoma. "Would you like me to pick up a coffee for you?"

She looked up from her typing and for a moment a smile flashed across her lips. "A tea, actually, if you would not mind, Mister Paradise."

It was nice to see her smile. "With milk?"

"And one sugar," she said. "Thank you."

Suddenly there was a dull popping sound followed by a thump as a splinter of wood jumped up from the floor.

"What was that?" she said.

"A gunshot!" I called back as I raced down the stairs. All I had feared, once I had seen them outside, was happening. I was always afraid that my investigative life could bring danger to those closest to me and now it had.

"I said, where is that big freak, old man," Manzetti's thug, Mickey, asked as he pointed a revolver at Mort. I burst into the store with all my speed so that by the time Mickey realized I was there and swung the gun to point at me I was within arm's length of him.

I grabbed the right hand holding the gun in my left hand, stopping the cylinder from revolving, and yanked hard, hearing a satisfying crack from his arm. He screamed in agony.

The gun discharged again as I stripped it away from him, the bullet this time going harmlessly into the floor.

"Damn you, freak!" Mickey managed when he could speak. His right arm hung limp and he dropped to his knees, his eyes watering.

His face still showed the results of the other night, his nose taped up and his left eye swollen.

I turned my attention to the other two with him. One I recognized as his friend Joey, who also showed the aftermath of the attack on me with a broken nose and two black eyes. The second thug with unlucky Mickey was a brown-haired, thin man, barely out of boyhood but with hard features and hooded, light brown eyes. He was dressed in the cheap blue suit that seemed to be a uniform for such thugs.

I saw him reach under his jacket, but he was across the room, and I would not be able to get to him before he drew the inevitable gun. He never got to, however, because Jake vaulted over the soda counter with a bottle of seltzer in his hand and slammed the bottle into the back of the gangster's head.

The thug dropped in a spray of carbonated water.

That left Joey suddenly standing very much alone in the middle of the store and very much aware of it.

I saw fear in his eyes and something else, confusion, perhaps?

"Stop now, Joey. Leave and get on a train out of town. Or you will lose that option." I left no room in my tone for doubt as to my meaning. He looked at the sobbing Mickey and the very unconscious third goon and decided he needed to be elsewhere. He moved to the door and left as fast as he could.

I addressed myself to the kneeling man. "I would give you the same advice, Mickey, but I know you're not bright enough to take it. So, I will tell you now; Manzetti will hear about this, and you know he will not be happy you brought a spotlight to his corner of the world. He likes the shadows."

I am not too sure he really understood everything I said but was pretty sure he got the general idea. I picked up his fallen gun and put it in my jacket pocket.

Then I turned my attention to a startled Mort and Jake. The store owner had a look of horror on his face but the soda-jerk, still crouching over the fallen thug, had shining eyes and a confused look on his features. The phantom shapes that swarmed around him were gold and black and grey, and to my eyes were like a swirling fog.

"What is this?" Mort said. "What is with guns? Gangsters!"

Not Born of Woman

"I'm so sorry," I said to Mort as I went over to Jake's side. "Easy, boy. It's over now."

The soda-jerk looked up at me and I saw the strange look fade out of his eyes and he was the freckle-faced boy again. He crossed himself in a silent blessing. "Gosh, Mister P," he said, "I just did that, didn't I?"

His breathing returned to normal, and I saw the adrenaline drop as his knees went rubbery. I put a hand on his shoulder and helped him to a stool just as the fallen man began to groan with returning consciousness.

"Easy, Jake," I said. "That was a very heroic act."

"Heroic?" Mort said. "That was *mshuga!*" His tone was reprimanding but he raced to the boy's side and put a fatherly arm around his shoulders.

I went back to the blubbering Mickey. "You better never cross my path again, Mickey. You have endangered my friends—I do not allow that to happen. Drag that thing with you out of here and crawl into a hole. I will speak with Manzetti. You can bet he will want to talk to you, and he will not be this courteous about it. If you have relatives far away, I'd visit them if I were you."

The broken thug went to the fallen one and, grabbing the jacket collar with his one good hand, half dragged, half walked the semi-conscious man to the entrance. I held the door open for him to exit just as Vandoma came out of my office entrance and entered the store.

"What happened?" she asked me as she looked at the two blood-covered gangsters now staggering into a sedan parked at the curb.

"Something that never should have," I said grimly. "Something I have always dreaded might." Then I turned back to make my apologies to Mort.

CHAPTER THIRTEEN

Mort had settled Jake down by the time I came over to them.

"I am sorry, Mort," I said. "This is because of me."

"No." Vandoma interposed herself between us. "It is because of me." She surveyed the shattered glass on the floor and looked up at the bullet hole in the ceiling and gave a little shudder. "It was because I asked Mister Paradise to recover something for me that such men as that have come here."

"No, Vandoma," I protested. "I am the one who didn't get a phone and was not specific about where my office was. I am so sorry, Mort. I will take my—"

"What, what?" the store owner said. "Don't talk nonsense, Adam. You help people, we all know that. You help the lady. You are not responsible for hoodlums like that."

"But I put you and Jake in harm's way."

"Hey, Mister P," the boy said. "I'm sorry if you think that, but we were the ones those would-be Dillingers were facing, and not for a minute do I blame you."

I was humbled by their words and looked from one to the other unable to speak.

"You two go back upstairs and let this lazy hero sweep up the mess he made," Mort said.

"And I will talk to you later about lessons, Adam." He looked to Vandoma.

I introduced the two of them.

Not Born of Woman

"Nice to meet you, Miss Kalderash," Mort added, "Though I wish it were under different circumstances." He smiled at her, and I was delighted to see that he ignored her hunchback, though he was clearly aware of it.

She shyly smiled at him, I suspect not used to many being so kind to a Roma.

I looked to Jake and put out a hand. "Thanks for the save, Jake. That was a brave thing."

He looked almost ashamed, and his cheeks colored, but his handshake was firm.

"It was the thing to do, sir," he said.

"Yes, it was, but many would not have. Thank you."

Vandoma and I exited the store and went back upstairs. When we got into the outer office, I closed the door behind us as she went to the desk to begin packing her things.

"What are you doing?" I asked.

"I have brought danger to you and to strangers," she said with a pained tone. "It is not good."

"Wait a minute," I said. "None of that is your fault. Like Mort said, it was the fault of those gangsters."

When she looked up at me from behind the desk her eyes were watery. She was clearly fighting tears. "No. No one should pay with their life for the foolishness of my brother. Those men had guns to kill you. You were attacked and I know it was from this. *Ez Rossz!*"

"No, this is not wrong," I said in answer to her Hungarian exclamation. "It is more than your brother's folly now. There is a killer involved in this somehow and there is no going back. Those fools downstairs are nothing, an exercise in male ego. No, your *Koshti Bok* is an object they want, but it is not the only thing. In fact, if we had not begun this investigation there is no way to know how far this would have gone."

"But you were hurt—"

"That is inconsequential," I said.

"No, it is not," she said with surprising energy. "I saw in your hand, I saw."

I felt a chill. "What did you see?"

She turned away from me, making a show of fussing with papers.

"Vandoma," I said sternly. "What did you see?"

When she looked at me there was a haunted quality in her dark eyes. "Your lifeline is like none I have ever seen ... and your heart line ... these things I do not understand. But I know that you are someone that is touched by *Devia*—the Universal God. Perhaps the *Baba Fingo*—the Savior." She said this all with eyes averted from me, her words vacillating between fear and reverence.

"What?" I felt as if there was a rock in my stomach. "No ... no ... I am not as any other man you may have met, but I am no more that than you are a *Sara e Kali*."

"A woman saint?" She said it with a bitter laugh, nodding to her hump. "You mock me."

"No," I declared. "Never. I, who am different from all others would never mock any, most especially you." I stepped closer to her but stayed on the opposite side of the desk, still conscious of my size. "Vandoma, the writer Mark Twain once said, 'The two most important days in your life are the day you are born and the day you find out why.' I remember my own birth but until now I was not sure of the why. I now know this is why: to help you."

She looked at me with confusion and I could see her thoughts went to what she had seen in my hands. I held those gloved hands out to her.

"Let me help you." We locked eyes.

"I saw many lives in your hands, many lifelines." She reached across and took my large, gloved hands in her smaller ones. "I do not know how that is so, but I saw no evil there. If you are not a *Beng*, a devil, what else can you be but the *Baba Fingo*?" Her voice was so quiet it was almost a whisper.

"Is it not enough that I am a friend? Look at me, I am not like others, but you did not fear me that first day. Do you really fear me now?"

She answered immediately. "No. I fear for you."

I had never heard such words and they frightened me in a way that neither Joey's knife nor the guns of the gangsters had. I knew for certain now I had to not only recover her family heirloom but stop whatever was compelling the Bundists or whoever had killed the pawnbroker.

Not Born of Woman

"I saw a great darkness," she continued. "And I saw what was life from death, and that puzzled me. So much danger and death and coldness."

"Believe. Together we can walk in the light on this," I said. "I will recover your *Koshti Bok* and more." I smiled and she returned it with a ghost of a one herself. "Now, no more talk of gods and devils. Man creates both in his own image, so let us fight the worst with the best."

She squeezed my hands for a moment then quickly returned to fussing with her papers, likely so I would not see her cry. I respected that and went into my office to look for my book of occult objects again.

I found it on a bookcase where I didn't remember putting it, but then I had been upset by her palm reading as she had been, so I must have set it down without a thought.

Now I sat down at the desk and began to look through the book again but had a hard time concentrating, at least until I heard the typewriter in the outer office going again.

Before I dug into the occult book, I pulled my journal from the bottom desk drawer and quickly jotted down my experiences from the night before. I liked to keep up to date and used the time to reflect on my daily progress in trying to find my purpose.

What had Vandoma really seen? Had she told me about my actual history with life from death? And how had I allowed myself to feel so connected to her? Eventually, I would have to move on, I would have to become someone after Adam Paradise when my time in New York was done. Yet, I meant what I said to her. I felt deeply that now I had found the thing I was born for—to help her and stop those blond thugs from obtaining the mystical talismans they were after. Such men could only use them for evil.

I seemed to have become involved in something bigger than I had ever imagined, something more than just a simple theft. The problems of the others whom I had helped before seemed to pale in comparison with the one that Vandoma had brought to me. Yet, I had to believe what Albert Camus said, "That men must live and create, and that Freedom was nothing but a chance to be better."

After I recorded my thoughts, I lost myself in reading about the various talismans in *Amuletae boni et mali* until quite some time later, when I was suddenly aware of voices in the outer office speaking quietly in Romani. I looked up to see Nico conversing in low tones with his sister.

He saw me look up and quieted, sending a dagger-sharp glance in my direction. He said goodbye to his sister and then left without looking back.

I closed the book and stepped into the outer office.

"I didn't mean to scare Nico off," I said. "I do not want to make trouble for you two."

"He has made the trouble," she said fiercely. "But he was ready to leave—he brought this." She handed me a list of the pawnshops that Tommy had given me with notations on a number of them.

"The tribe has been to all those marked," she said. "Those"—she pointed to some with Xs—"and the checks mean they are dealers who would have the sort of objects you asked about."

"And these that are circled?"

She smiled. "They are the ones my brother said are criminals for certain. And he knows such things." She laughed a little sad laugh. "Too well."

"This will be a very good start," I said. "It will save me a lot of time with this list of fences."

"Fences?"

"Dealers in stolen goods. Whomever took your *Koshti Bok* from Dorfman will want to turn it into cash; I know for sure now that the Nazis did not take it."

"How do you know this?"

Uh oh, just when I got her calmed down, I opened the door to tell her about last night. Well, she deserves to know the truth.

I told her, in an abbreviated and sanitized form, about my encounter with Hans and his friends from last night. I saw anger flare in her eyes.

"It is not good that you are in such danger," she said. "This is why I wished you to—"

"I know," I said. "But you must understand, this is what I have accepted, and it is what must be done to recover your *Koshti Bok*. And, as I said, this is much bigger now as well and I am involved whether I wanted to be or not."

"You will be careful?" It came off more like an order than a question and I nodded.

"As I can, at all times," I said. "I have both good luck and good purpose now."

"What will you do now?"

"A bit late today, but I'll hit each of these circled ones tomorrow and see if I can get a little heat going."

She raised her eyebrows. "Heat?"

"Sorry, yes, if I poke a stick into enough burrows, eventually a rat will come out."

"I do not like that."

"When one has no leads, sometimes the thing to do is to make the leads come to me."

"Like those of the bent cross who came to you last night?" she said accusingly.

"Well, I learned in the negative they did not steal it. So, that's something."

From her look, she was not very convinced, but before we could continue her examination of my investigation methods the door to the outer office opened and a uniformed policeman stepped into the room.

He froze for a second when he saw me, a reaction I had seen before and was used to but recovered quickly.

"Adam Paradise?"

"Yes."

"Detective Shane put a call over the radio car for you to come with me, please."

"What's wrong, officer?"

"There's been a death, Mister Paradise."

Vandoma gave a little gasp.

"Do you know who?"

"I think Detective Shane would like to tell you himself," he said but from his grim expression, I knew it was serious.

I looked to Vandoma. "I'll take care of this and—"

"I will wait here until you return." she said with no uncertainty. "I have much work to do."

"Okay," I said. "I'll be back as soon as I can—or send word through Jake downstairs."

"I will wait."

She was a very determined person.

"As you wish. I'll see you later."

I grabbed my hat and coat and followed the officer with a sick feeling in the pit of my stomach.

CHAPTER FOURTEEN

The officer—O'Brien by name—didn't speak much as we drove in his black and white squad car across town and that sinking feeling in the pit of my stomach grew from a pebble to a stone. We went up the west side of Manhattan to West End Avenue and Seventy-Ninth Street, near the boat basin.

The car pulled up in front of a pawnshop on the corner of Seventy-Ninth. There were two other black and white units out front and several uniformed officers standing around.

"Glad you were in the office, Adam," Tommy said to me, offering a hand to shake. "Sorry to be dramatic, but it was easier to put the call over the radio than calling the drugstore and trying to find you that way."

"I'm glad I was there," I said. "And you're right, this was faster." Taking in the police presence and the grim looks I asked, "What are we looking at?"

He escorted me through the front door of the pawnshop into a room that looked like a tornado had hit it. The showroom of the shop had the usual knicknacks and items for sale scattered all around, jewelry, Victrolas, glassware, and even furniture crushed nearly to pulp. Breakfronts and glass display cases were all shattered and every step crunched as we walked in.

There was a photographer changing the plate in a box camera when we entered.

"I finished in the back, Tommy, and just about done out here," the photographer said. "I'm gonna need a stiff one after this." He was too busy to even look up at me, but I could see the normally stoic police photographer and even the other officers in the room all were pale.

"This is a bad one, Adam," Tommy said. "I just wanted to prepare you."

That shocked me as my friend knew I had seen some very bad things—though he had no idea the true extent of my experiences prior to New York.

He led me through a curtain to the back of the store where we stopped just beyond. We were in a back room that had been a parlor of the apartment behind the storefront. It had been the storeowner's home. Now it was a charnel house.

The smell of death permeated the room, which, if anything was in even worse shape than the showroom had been. Only here there was the swirling crimson-tinged black cloud hovering over the remains of one middle-aged man who was horribly dead in the middle of the room. His shirtless body, with his face locked in an eternal look of horror, was tied by a rope around his chest to a tipped-over chair, resting on his side.

I spotted the fingers of his tied hands that were clearly broken, and the chest of the victim cut and burned in a clear case of torture—then tipped over and carelessly discarded like a doll. There was blood everywhere.

We paused in the doorway with both the sight and smell striking both of us powerfully. Tommy was right to warn me for it was as bad as anything I had ever seen, though I did not realize it would get worse.

"As far as we can tell," my friend said, "That is the remains of Adolph Gartz, owner-proprietor of this place. Neighbors said he's lived and worked here for twenty-something years."

I looked at Tommy questioningly. "Does this have anything to do with Dorfman?"

He waved me forward. "The room's been photographed and printed, so you can look closer—if you want. And yes, I think it does."

I took him at his word and went to kneel where the arm—the left—was lying exposed beneath his body. It was clear that, like Dorfman, all the fingers had been methodically broken. From my knees, I could also

Not Born of Woman

see a small safe visible across the room that had been concealed in the bottom of a breakfront. It was open and empty.

"So, another series killer?" I asked. He nodded his head.

"Look in the next room," he said in a tone that chilled me. Then he added, "It's worse."

He was right. A short corridor led to two back bedrooms. To the left was obviously the owner's room, with heavy masculine furniture, now in disarray, but the one to the right was clearly feminine in softer hues with lace curtains. The room's pinks were stained red now, as the body of a young girl, a Bobbysoxer, was on the center of the flowered bedspread.

It was a horrific sight.

She had been spread-eagled on the bed and tied to the four corners, fully clothed, but had her throat slit. Her wide green eyes were eternally staring in terror at the ceiling. Her red hair was splayed out on the bed like a halo. Indeed, she was an angel now.

The crimson-tinged shape that hovered over her was deep indigo, streaked with slashes of black. Hers had been a horrible death.

"My gods," I muttered. "This is connected to the missing girls?"

"Yes," he said. "Details we did not let out in the papers."

"Which are?"

He turned away from the horrible scene and spoke with his back to me. "The girl is Rebecca Gartz, the old man's granddaughter, living with him since her parents died in a car crash ten years ago."

I stepped closer to look at the poor girl. There were symbols written in blood on her forehead. Alchemical symbols I recognized from my readings, though I did not know what they meant.

"You see that stuff on her forehead?" Tommy said, "The girl we found last week had the same thing. And there was another girl found two weeks ago we didn't let get out. Same."

I stared at her face. I did my best to memorize it. Life to one such as I was a precious thing. I often felt that too many took it for granted, that to live was a right, but I knew it was not. It was a gift. And that gift had been taken from this young girl and that man in the front, torn from them in the worst way. I had indeed become embroiled in something much bigger than the theft of a family heirloom.

I thought of Dante Alighieri again. "I am the way into the city of woe, I am the way into eternal pain, I am the way to go among the lost."

The girl looked like so many young girls I saw each day that she seemed almost familiar.

"How many more, Tommy?"

"Four bodies over the last two months, only the last one the papers caught wind of. There have been three other girls gone missing who fit the description, but we have not found them yet."

"What else?" I asked. "The things that connect them?"

"Good students, good girls." He said with disgust, "All high school age. All with those marks—"

"They are alchemical symbols."

"What?"

"Things the old magicians would write when they tried to do things like turn lead to gold," I said. "Or to create life from inanimate objects."

"Damn," he said. "It keeps getting worse."

We left the room and walked outside to the street to get some sorely needed fresh air.

"You see why I got you up here," Tommy said. "Dorfman and now this—it is connected for sure and seems to cross into the missing girls." He lit a cigarette and inhaled deeply as if the smoke could clear the smell of death or the images of what he had just seen from his mind.

At that point, I realized there would be no way to keep Vandoma and the reason I was involved in this out of the case, but I could at least give her a heads up about it.

"You gonna tell me how you really got into this?" Tommy asked me.

"You psychic?" I asked. "I was just thinking about that very thing."

"Well?"

"I need to tell my client I am going to open up on this," I said. "But I will tell you and bring any and all that I have on it to you tomorrow."

"Morning?"

"Absolutely," I said. "First thing. I have to get some notes from my office anyway, but I owe it to my client to at least let them know things may tie in—but I guarantee you their involvement is tangential to this thing. I was trying to recover an object stolen from them recently, which is how I got to Dorfman. That is as far as it goes."

"You're on a thin limb on this one, Adam."

"I've never lied or let you down before. I won't this time."

"Okay," he said. "First thing, though."

"Promise."

"You want a squad car to drop you home?"

"My office, if you don't mind," I said. "I have something to take care of there."

"But the police will say we did these horrible things," Vandoma said. "They always say 'Gypsies are criminals.'"

"Not this time, I promise." I had explained all I had seen, not holding back, to impress her with the importance of my informing Tommy about everything. "You met my friend; he is a fair man. Somehow, your *Koshti Bok* is now important to this killer."

"How can that be? Did not these deaths begin before Nico did this foolish thing?"

"I agree," I said, "which is why I know Tommy will have no reason to think your involvement is anything but incidental. Still, the list of the pawnshops that your brother narrowed down for us could help the police—and it seems only fair since he gave me the list, to begin with."

She knit her brows and I could see that this was a hard thing for her. I knew that family reputation was important, but here distrust of the police was deep seated.

"I don't care about my license, which could easily get pulled from me if I don't talk to him," I said honestly, "but while I have an obligation to protect you as my client as much as I can, I also feel an obligation to help stop a killer."

"Yes, that is a good thing, but this is now a family matter," she said after some time. "I must speak to my mother. I can no longer keep from her what Nico has done."

"I am sorry for that, Vandoma, I would have protected you from having to reveal this, but—"

"No, Mister Paradise," she said, working to smile, though it was a sad one. She had packed her work for the day before I returned and so she stood up and grabbed her coat and bag with the manuscript she had typed in it. "I knew after that first day that it might come to this, to have to tell my mother. And it is not for me that I worry, it is for her. And for the honor of the Kalderash name."

"I think I should be there when you tell your mother," I said.

"Yes," she said. "This would be good, so she will understand why it is important. It would be good if my brother would be there as well, for he must face what he has done."

"Okay then," I said. "Let's lock up and get a taxi."

CHAPTER FIFTEEN

Vandoma, Nico, and their mother lived in an A-frame house in Long Island City in the Burrough of Queens. We took the Fifty-Ninth Street Bridge from the upper Eastside. Normally, Vandoma said she took the trolley over the bridge and then the train to downtown Manhattan so balked at the cost of the taxi, but I put her mind at ease.

"Think of it as a convenience for me," I said. "My leg is still a bit sore, especially since I had to do a lot of walking last night." Whether she believed me or just humored me, she did not bring it up again.

We rode in silence.

I tried to imagine how she felt, knowing she would be admitting to her mother that she had not guarded the *Koshti Bok* well enough. And more the shame of her brother actually using it for a gambling debt. On top of that, bringing in an outsider—me—and now the police. I could feel her inner turmoil though she presented a calm surface. She was in great discomfort. And it pained me that I could not help more.

When we arrived at the modest home in a semi-rural, semi-industrial area of Queens we stood in front of the cottage nervously, each for our own reasons.

"My mother does not have many visitors," she finally said. "So, it is best I go in first." She pulled her coat tightly around her against a sudden gust of wind and moved ahead of me to insert her key in the door.

"Mother," she called in Hungarian as she opened the door. "I have come with company."

From inside the house, a reedy voice called back in Hungarian, "Why would you bring a stranger to this home?"

"It is a necessity," Vandoma called back. She led me into a small closed-in porch where she hung up her coat on a clothes tree and I followed suit, hanging my hat over the trench coat but keeping on my gloves.

The inner door from the foyer was open and we stepped up into a hallway with a sitting room off to the left, and a stairway off to the right going up to the second story.

"Go into the parlor," the voice called from straight ahead in a lighted room that looked to be the kitchen. "I will join you there."

The parlor was decorated in the old style, with heavy wooden furniture, throw rugs and a fireplace whose mantel had an old, Viennese clock on it. The curtains on the windows were heavy red velvet.

"Please have a seat," Vandoma said, waving to an overstuffed chair on one side of the hearth. It was narrow enough that I had to wedge myself into it. Vandoma sat in a matching chair on the other side of the hearth, looking dwarfed in hers.

"I will tell her," she said. "I—"

"Introduce me, daughter," a grey-haired woman as small as Vandoma said. She was an older version of her daughter, but thinner and standing straight.

"Mother," Vandoma said, rising, "this is Mister Adam Paradise."

I rose and was surprised when my size did not register any fright in the older woman's eyes.

Vandoma is her mother's daughter.

"Mrs. Kalderash," I said, speaking in Hungarian. "It is a pleasure to meet you."

"I am sorry the man of the house, my son Nico is not here to greet you." The old woman gave a welcoming smile. "You are the man who my daughter makes the typing for?" She moved to sit in a rocker and motioned for us both to sit as well.

"No, Mama," Vandoma said. I saw her summon her strength as she continued in Romani. "I have hired Mister Paradise to retrieve the *Koshti Bok*, which Nico has given to a gambler for a debt."

Not Born of Woman

The old woman kept a stoic face, but I saw her eyes go to me and then back to Vandoma with a flare of fire in them. "Why have you done this? How could your brother do such a thing?" She and Vandoma spoke in Romani, and I decided it would be in the best interests of all concerned if I did not let on to the older woman that I understood their language.

"Nico has the *gadjo* sickness of gambling," Vandoma said, "and it is greater than his adherence to the old ways. He took the *Koshti Bok* to pay a debt and it was stolen from those to whom he gave it. This man knows the *gadjo* world and undertook to find it for me."

"Why would he do that?" Her mother asked with suspicion and an implication.

"Because I asked him," Vandoma said.

"And how will you pay for such a thing?" There was a bitter and accusatory note in the old woman's tone. "The Kalderash do not stoop to—"

"Nor would I," Vandoma said in a suddenly sharp retort. "He is a good man. He has asked only a meal in payment, nothing more."

"This is family business," her mother insisted. "You were not right to go outside the family—and to a *gadjo*."

"It is not just family business anymore," Vandoma said. "There have been deaths connected to this." She proceeded to give her mother a sanitized, but accurate, version of what we knew about the circumstances that were swirling around the stolen heirloom.

The old woman digested this information with stony silence, her eyes occasionally looking to me as I sat there pretending not to understand what was being said. When Vandoma had concluded the recitation of events, her mother looked at me and her eyes narrowed.

"Why do you wish to help my daughter, *gadjo*?" she asked me in Hungarian. "Your kind does not do anything but for gain."

"Mother!"

"No, Miss Kalderash," I said in Hungarian. "Your mother is right; everyone wants something. I do have something to gain, Mrs. Kalderash."

She stared at me as if seeing me for the first time. She indicated with a jerk of her finger for me to come closer. I stood and walked across the room and stopped a foot or so away from her.

She looked up at me, squinting and I realized her eyes were not so good and she had not really seen me except in a general way before. Now she scrutinized me with some shock.

"*Coxani!*" she whispered. It was the Romani word for witch, male or female.

"No," I said, noticing her surprise when I clearly understood what she said. "No more than you, who can see 'that which is.'"

She looked quickly to her daughter, who nodded and said, "Yes, he speaks our language."

"I am shamed," the old woman said in Romani.

"No, Mother Kalderash," I said. "You have no reason for shame—you said nothing that is not true. The *gadjo* world is a greedy one. The *Romani* have had to make their own way in that hostile world. And yes, I want something—besides doing what is right and helping someone who is in need—which in the *Rromani* way should be enough. I wish to *Parrujmos*—to barter with her. All I wish is a good *Roma* meal. I don't get home cooking very often."

She looked at me with incredulity, but her expression changed when she made a gesture that I recognized as a warding sign. "I wish to see you," she said. And I knew she meant to open herself to view me with a psychic eye.

Vandoma said her mother had the sight besides being a healer.

After my experience with her daughter reading my palms, I had feared this, for I had no idea what she would discover about me. Would she see the phantoms that hovered around me as I saw them around others, for the dead that supplied my limbs and body had never left me? Like the essence of humanity that swirled around the mob's killers and the Bund, I too had my own ghostly "moons" in orbit, though I was so used to them that I essentially took no notice anymore.

"I must look," she said.

"No, Mother," Vandoma protested. "This is a violation."

"No," I said, "it is all right, Miss Kalderash. This is the only way your mother will know she can trust me."

Not Born of Woman

I took off my gloves and held out my hands to the old woman. "I am here to be seen."

There was a long moment before she reached up and took my hands. I felt a strange tingling sensation surge up from my hands when her delicate fingers touched mine.

"How are you called?" she said. I knew it was a formal request, a ritual calling.

"I am called Adam Paradise." At least I was now. I had always been Adam, though I have—when I needed a different second name—used other last names. Milton's poem had always appealed to me, so I had been Providence, Shepherd, and others at different times. Yet I had always been Adam and now before this woman, I opened myself. "I am always Adam."

This distinction seemed to matter to her, and she tilted her head. I saw her eyes unfocus as she looked not at me, but into me. She began to make a low hum, from deep inside her. This was not the "gypsy fortune telling" of the movies and books, not a show for some *booja*—some trick. That was a *gicsvara*, a hustler. This was from the old ways, from traditions that were corrupted or lampooned by the western culture that had demonized the Roma. It was both an honor and, for me, a frightening experience that she did this looking in.

The old woman's eyes seemed to glow with lambent light and her focus sharpened as she looked me directly in the eyes. "*Mullo*," she said in a whisper. It was the Romani word for "spirits of the dead"—what most would call a revenant, the undead.

I heard Vandoma gasp.

"Why do you walk this world?" she asked, though there was no fear in her voice. "You are of *Martja* as well, the spirit of death yet you walk among us as one of the living?"

"I do not know my purpose," I said honestly. "Except to learn. I remember the moment I awoke, and I was as I am now. It has been my *baxt*—my luck—to be here at this time. And I would make it a better place while I strive to understand why I am here."

"All are here to understand why," she said. "Yet none are as you." She brought my hands to hold them pressed firmly to her cheeks. "Death, yet life. This is something only told in the stories."

"Mother," Vandoma said. "You cannot mean—"

"Yes," the elder Kalderash said. "I feel no evil here, this is a *pajivalo* being such as the legends speak."

Pajivalo meant honorable in the *Romani* tongue, but what legend she spoke of I dared not speculate.

"A *gadjo* lord once sought to steal power from *Devel*, the universal one, and made life from death—creating a creature neither man nor demon, neither alive nor dead. But this *gadjo mullo* would not obey his creator, hearing the voice of the Devel and fled from this world to return to the great dark."

She was telling my story. My story!

As the reality had become a legend of the Frankenstein family that was taken and altered into the story by Mary Shelly, so the legend had been told among the Roma of Eastern Europe. And now was being told back to me. I had lived—if live I do—in fear of this moment, of my reality being revealed, yet now that it had been put out in the open and before Vandoma, I felt a great sense of relief.

"I know this story," I said quietly. "I have lived it, and I live it still. It is my story."

Both women gave an intake of breath that was so simultaneous it might have been choreographed. Yet the old woman did not pull back from me. She stared at me, and her features softened.

"I have *ladz*," she said. "Shame for questioning. This is the destiny of the three sisters of fate who have brought you here. My son has given away the *Koshti Bok*, and now you have come to help return it to us."

"*Solax*," I said in Romani, "I take an oath. I will return your *Koshti Bok* and do all I can to defend the Kalderash honor." She kissed my fingertips.

"*Cinavas*, I agree," she said. "We have a bargain." She rose and looked to her daughter.

"Vandoma, show the gentleman out and come make me some tea." She nodded to me and then tottered out of the room, taking with her a palpable energy and leaving the two of us a bit confused.

CHAPTER SIXTEEN

Vandoma did not seem to know what to say as she walked with me to the door of their home. I stood outside for a long moment, holding my hat, and feeling awkward. I remembered a quote from Paradise Lost and said, "'And chiefly Thou, O Spirit, that dost prefer, Before all Temples th' upright heart and pure, Instruct me.'"

She looked at me oddly then gave a quizzical smile. "I will return to type tomorrow," she said. "Then if your policeman wishes to ask things of me, I will answer."

"Thank you, Vandoma. I will do my best to keep you out of it as much as I can."

"I know. Good night, Mister Paradise. Be careful."

"I always am," I lied. I saw a disapproving look and added, "Alright, I will from this moment on." This got a smile from her and a wave. That made me feel heartened.

On the trolley ride across the bridge, I realized that there was a good chance Hans and his cronies would be waiting for me at my apartment. It behooved me then, to take the battle to them, so to speak.

So, when I arrived in Manhattan, I made a phone call from a payphone to Digger.

"I wanted to thank you again for the *Amuletae boni et mali*," I said. "It's nice light reading." That made him laugh.

"My pleasure," he said. "Your timing is good; I was just going to close the shop."

"I'm afraid I have another request," I said. When I told him what I wanted he said, "Just a minute." I heard him rustling papers in the background and in less time than I thought it was possible, he was back on the phone.

"Okay, Adam," he said. "I have exactly what you asked for, but you really shouldn't mess with those guys."

"I have no choice," I said, "they messed with me first."

"Ah," he said. "'The supreme art of war is to subdue the enemy without fighting.'"

"Sun Tzu," I retorted to his implied challenge. "True, but Tolstoy said, 'The two most powerful warriors are patience and time.' I've run out of patience for this."

"Let's hope you don't run out of time."

While I was in Chinatown, on the edge of Little Italy, I decided that another visit to Guido Manzetti was in order. I was not surprised that there were two new monolithic henchmen seated at a back table but was astonished when I entered and I was not challenged.

Instead, Manzetti waved me over and as I sat, a waiter brought a cappuccino that he set before me. I acknowledged the gesture and sipped.

"It is very difficult to find reliable help," the little, balding loan shark said. He was still enveloped with the swirling, deep purple and crimson shades of the many dead souls that were connected to him.

"I did notice you have two new watchdogs."

"Yes." He did not look up from his own cup, as if he was reading the swirling black of the liquid. "Some guys do things in their off-hours that complicate things."

"One can't control what employees do in their off-hours."

Not Born of Woman

"Former employees," he said quietly. He puffed on a thin cigarette, which I noticed was hand-rolled with great delicacy.

"Still, actions not on the employer, current or former."

"Kind of you." He looked up. "So, we're even."

"Cleanly and on good terms."

He nodded.

"You are a professional, sir," I said as I started to stand. "Always comforting to do business with professionals."

"Then I would like to ask something of you — professionally." This stopped me and I settled back. Would this be the vig — the interest, even though he had said we were even.

"If I can, Mister Manzetti."

"There is a priest in Chelsea."

"Father Burton?"

"Yes." He stubbed out his cigarette in a crystal ashtray on the table that had a dozen stubs in it. "I don't go to church much anymore, but my mother, she does. And I got a cousin who is a priest up in Rochester."

He paused and brought out the fixings to roll another cigarette with surprising deftness. When he was done, he put the cigarette to his lips and one of the new bodyguards was suddenly at the table with a gold lighter to ignite it. Just as quickly we two were alone again and Manzetti took a long drag before he spoke. "It is a bad thing for everyone when people feel that priests can be hurt."

"Yes," I said. "I agree. My friend Tommy Shane and lots of his professional friends have that same feeling as well."

"That's good." He nodded slightly and sipped his cappuccino. I sensed he was happy he wasn't asking me to do anything I was not doing already, so no new obligations were being accrued. "Nice to know the community is of one mind."

"Yes," I said. "I know it might not seem like it — as if I were on two jobs — but it seems now that both things are really connected —"

"As many things in the world are."

"Indeed, Mister Manzetti," I observed. "Machiavelli said, 'He who wished to be obeyed must know how to command.' I'll make sure I keep to my task."

"'It is not titles that honor men, but men that honor titles.'" He quoted the Italian prince back to me and then said. "Have a nice night, Mister Paradise."

He emphasized "mister." I took that as a compliment. I tipped my hat and left.

Things were indeed getting interesting.

The Bund's national headquarters was located at 178 East Eighty-Fifth Street. It was a four-story townhouse sandwiched in between a taller apartment house and several other townhouses, some of which had ground-floor storefronts. There was a huge Swastika flag hanging from a pole out front and a lot of blond types walking in and out of the building.

You would think it would be hard to hide a seven-foot-plus figure, even in New York, but I have become good at going unobserved despite my size and appearance. I have learned to blend in for it seems to be a matter of mindfulness and attitude.

It was twilight now and there was a deep doorway across the street where I was able to secrete myself.

I watched the building for a time, observing the lights going on or off in the various rooms visible from the street. There was no unusual activity beyond the comings and goings of many angry-looking men—far too many for my taste. In the late afternoon, there was a delivery of a large trunk that two strong men carried into the building from a panel truck.

As the night deepened, traffic into the building lessened and finally, by ten o'clock there was no more traffic and few lights on in the building. The ground floor was still active, but the third and fourth floors were all dark.

I consulted the sketch of the layout of the building that Digger had made when I stopped at his store; the depth of his knowledge seemed bottomless. I was fairly certain Hans' rooms were on the fourth floor where the movers and shakers of the Bund had living quarters. I determined that it would be best to use the roof as my entry point.

To that end, once the street was empty, I crossed to the apartment building next to the Bund headquarters and gained access, moving quickly through the first floor to the back courtyard.

I climbed a backyard fence and made my way to the Bund's backyard unobserved. I then climbed up at the corner of the building, out of sight of any windows. It was easy with the rough brick construction, so I made quick but careful progress toward the roof. The almost full moon was dancing in and out of the clouds and served to conceal me from any who might glance out of nearby buildings.

As I climbed, I thought again about why it was that I did this, what part of me demanded that I pursue trouble, even risk that greatest of all gifts—my life. Perhaps it was just a need to prove to myself why I did not die in the cold. Why had I been brought to life and allowed to continue to have consciousness at all? My creator, Victor, had brought me into being for selfish reasons, as an exercise in his own hubris. Now, in an effort to make that life mean something I did what I did.

After all, what was it that made me different from the bovines slaughtered for meat? I had consciousness and with that the ability (or was it a curse?) to question my place in the scheme of the Great Creator's plan. Most life was driven by its own limitations. It was foreknowledge that death was inevitable that propelled humankind to attempt to accomplish something, to leave a mark, a legacy. I had no idea how long my lifespan would or could be. Would I continue until the sun dimmed or one day suddenly cease to be, returning to the dust of the dead from which I had been conjured?

I was a 'thing' created—life from death—animate from inanimate—yet, parts of whom had once been animate. A breathing paradox. And apparently, a living legend. Or myth.

The old Roma woman spoke of me as something more than the fiction most people accepted, the morality play/parable that Mary Shelly had shaped. Mother Kalderash made it clear that I was the embodiment of a fireside tale. But to scare children, or to give hope to the old that life would always triumph even out of death?

In some the thing that drove them day to day, beyond the mechanical needs of food and rest, was a desire to leave a legacy in the world, to perhaps make it a better place than they found it. In others what drove them was to grasp in desperation at each breath with no thought to the future, no care for others or posterity.

For now, I would settle for a simple goal—to aid Vandoma in recovering her family's luck and claim a home-cooked meal. And, perhaps to inconvenience men like the fascists who would steal hope from others for the sake of their own greed for power. Either goal would suffice to keep me motivated for one more day of my Quixotic life.

As I neared the roof, but before I could climb over the edge, I became aware of a flickering glow and the sound of multiple voices chanting in German. This caused me to stop my ascent and listen.

I heard the words *Zigeuner*, which was the word for a Romani in native German, and *Kushti Bok*. My curiosity drove me to inch upward and I peered over the edge. On the flat roof, surrounded by torches, were half a dozen of the Bund members dressed in scarlet robes incised with runes.

They had apparently just concluded some sort of ritual around a flaming brazier. One of the members moved to cover the metal brazier with a lid and smother the flame. When it was done, they all lowered their cowl-like hoods. One of them was Hans.

"We cannot find full power until the moon is full, according to the texts," one of the others said to their leader, "so it seems pointless to recite these words without a subject."

Hans gave him a nasty look. "We practice to achieve perfection," the blond leader said. "It is *Herr* Himmler's paramount and most perfect command. To achieve order, we must strive for perfection. Whether or not we retrieve the artifact—we may still proceed with the other things we have. It is sure we have all we need for the spell to work. Though redundancies are to be hoped for. Regardless, we will have a weapon to subdue these weak Americans and rally the pure to our cause. A new, glorious age will dawn."

"But will we be able to find this thing?"

"Never doubt," Hans counseled. "We will find that freak and whoever helped him escape us and then, with him out of the way, proceed as planned." He clapped his comrade on the shoulder and gave a cheery smile. "Come, let us have a drink and look over the plans for the rally at Siegfried; I still hope to be able to perform the ceremony then. If we find that object by then, so much the better, but we have the other talismans."

The group vacated the roof and, after waiting to be sure they had left, I eased myself up onto the tar-papered surface.

Two tiki-type torches still burned, but it was clear they would sputter themselves out soon, so the Bundists apparently hadn't thought it necessary to extinguish them. This allowed me a clear view of the whole space.

The brazier was in the center of an area with painted markings on the wooden plank floor, occult symbols I had seen in a number of books—Norse Runes. If there had been any doubt that the Bundists were acquiring occult objects for their own purposes, the use of the runes removed that.

They practice but for what? Not some idle, scholarly investigation, that is certain.

Whatever their goal or what coming ceremony they were alluding to, neither was my investigation that night. I was determined to have a reckoning with the Nazi leader and to that end I followed the robed figures down the stairs into their lair.

CHAPTER SEVENTEEN

The staircase led down to a corridor on the top floor of the building that was lined with doors but there was no indication which of the doors Hans was behind. I could hear the Bundists on the lower floors talking and milling around, and if he had gone down to them my purpose would be blunted.

From the floor plan I had looked over at Digger's, I had the idea that the largest of the suites on this floor would be at the opposite end. From his ego, I was sure that would be Hans' room. I walked down the hall alert and ready to encounter trouble.

A door to my right opened abruptly and a blond fellow in his early twenties stepped out, his eyes going wide when he saw me. I wasted no time in conversation and slapped him with a backhand blow that sent him flying back into the room where he lay on the floor unmoving. It was a dorm-like room with a single bed. I pulled the door closed, confident he would not wake for some time.

At the last door on the corridor, I listened for a moment and heard the sound of occupancy.

"I think we need to deal with that *riesen jude* tomorrow; it's important." Hans' voice was harsh and commanding. "We must find out who helped him and punish them as well."

"We will, Hans," another voice said, "but you'll never get any rest if you keep on like this. Let's have a drink and relax. He can't escape us once we start looking."

"But he must be made to pay, and others must be made to know of it." Hans continued, "Himmler was wise when he said, 'The best political weapon is the weapon of terror. Cruelty commands respect. Men may hate us. But, we don't ask for their love; only for their fear.'" There was laughter following that and the clinking of glasses.

I had heard enough. I tried the doorknob, but it was locked. So, I knocked.

"What?" called an annoyed voice from inside.

"Message for *Herr* Hans Schmidt," I said, doing my best to disguise my voice. "It is important."

"Alright." Footsteps approached, and I heard the distinctive clicking sound as the door was unlocked.

As the portal opened, I surged forward, slamming the individual opening the door with my shoulder so that he flew into a wall and dropped, unmoving. I reached past the first man to a second figure, who I grabbed around the throat. He was of a kind with the others, blond, muscular, and arrogant featured. I squeezed his neck until his eyes bulged and he went blue. He fell from my grasp unconscious—or possibly dead—at that point, I did not care.

Hans was standing across the parlor room of his suite. He froze with a brandy bottle in hand. He made a strangled sound when he saw his colleagues drop and made to throw the bottle at me.

I kicked the door closed behind me and swatted the bottle aside in midair as it came at my head. I was across the room before he could cry out and fastened my hands around the Bund leader's throat.

"You wanted to find me, *Herr* Schmidt?" I said. "This *riesen* is here now. You have something to say to me?"

The Bundist's eyes bulged, and I was forced to let up the pressure on his throat enough for him to draw a breath to speak.

"You will pay for this, you *mischling*," Hans croaked.

"You will stop your pursuit of the mystical items," I said. "You will cease your hateful ways, or I will be very unhappy."

"Why should I care that you are happy or not, Gypsy-loving swine," he spat, suddenly not the least afraid. I suppose he felt protected by his ideology of superiority. I decided to make sure he knew he was not.

"You should learn to care what other people think, Nazi," I said, intentionally lowering my voice to a near growl. "If you wish to live in this world you will have to live with them."

"Not if we have our way." He was unrepentant and defiant.

I did not like that.

I reached out with my left hand and casually snapped his right arm over my knee.

Hans yelped in pain but glared at me with hate. Through clenched teeth, he hissed, "You will suffer for this, *mischling*!"

"Then hear this mongrel, Nazi. You like so much to quote Germans, so listen to a quote from your countryman Nietzsche: 'To live is to suffer, to survive is to find some meaning in the suffering.'" I lifted him so that his feet dangled and leaned in to lock eyes with him. "Find a different meaning, Nazi, or I will be back."

I saw in his face that he would not heed my warning, so I broke his other arm.

He fainted then.

I dropped him to the floor. I was more disgusted than I had ever been. I had hoped to put a stop to their Bundist ways before it got worse, but I could see that was not possible. His ideology was a cankerous one. Shakespeare might well have been describing him when he wrote, "It is a tale told by an idiot, full of sound and fury; signifying nothing."

I left the Bundists where they fell and went out the way I had come in, having accomplished nothing.

I chose to go to my office instead of my apartment after my disappointing meeting with the Nazis. It seemed that self-preservation was the only thing some people understood—they seemed to have no empathy at all for others and their suffering. The ideology of hate that the National Socialist Bund seemed to hold as a core principle was a hard one for me to understand.

Not Born of Woman

I knew that mankind had always demonized "the other"—any group or individual that was different—and usually out of fear of the mainstream group's own weaknesses. The American writer Lovecraft said, "The oldest and strongest emotion of mankind is fear, and the oldest and strongest kind of fear is fear of the unknown."

But Hans Schmidt and his confederates were not poverty-stricken, not physically sick or downtrodden, so I could not see their justification for the fear and hate that was so deeply ingrained in the Bundists.

I pondered all this as I walked up the stairs to my office. I knew I would not sleep, so thought some reading of the book from Digger might calm me. At the top of the stairs, I paused, as there was a light on in the empty office at the back of the building that Mort used for storage. That was strange, as the store below had been closed for several hours.

I moved as quietly as I could to the back office, alert after my encounters with Joey and the Bundists. I wondered if someone had planned to ambush me in the morning and had not counted on me returning that night.

There was only a soft sound from within the room, a soft scratching. After a moment of listening, I grasped the doorknob and burst into the storage room.

"What!" A very startled Mort jumped up from a desk, an old-style quill pen in his hand. On the desk in front of him, in a cleared space surrounded by boxes was a large book. "Oh, Adam!"

"I'm sorry, Mort," I said. "I didn't think—"

"Oh, not to worry, son," he said. "I just came up to do inventory—I've been putting it off for too long."

He settled down to the seat he'd been in and closed the large leather-covered book and the inkwell he was using for his quill pen. When he saw my look at the quill he smiled.

"I am old-fashioned, my friend," he said. "I don't like those new-style fountain pens. They always clog up on me." He laughed. "Using the feather makes me feel like a scribe instead of just a simple storekeeper."

The room, which I had never been in before, was still appointed as an office much like mine, but with boxes stacked around in a seemingly haphazard manner. Again, he saw my gaze.

"I know it looks *mishuga*, Adam, but Jake follows direction well enough, and we have a system." He waved around and pointed. "Corn-plasters, bicarbonate, light bulbs, and such. I keep any drugs downstairs, but this lets me stay well stocked."

"Well, I'm sorry to break your concentration," I said.

"Not to worry," he replied. He capped his inkwell and stretched theatrically. "I'd lost track of time, so it is good to say enough for the night."

I accompanied him out into the hall and waited while he locked the office door. He walked me down to mine.

"So, tomorrow, Adam, perhaps we begin your Hebrew lessons?"

"I would like that, Mort," I said. "How is say, six o'clock?"

"That is good," he said as he headed down the stairs. "You should get some rest."

"Look who's talking, Mort. But I will only work a little and promise to get some rest. Good night."

I opened my office and walked into the foyer, finding it oddly reassuring to see Vandoma's typewriter sitting on what I now thought of as her desk.

I have not had this many attachments to either people or places in my time previously among mankind. It confuses things and I can't afford to be confused—it is more than the Koshti Bok now. There are deaths connected to this.

In my office, I found the *Amuletae boni et mali* where I'd left it—the page marker that I had carefully placed at the edge of the book was now at the spine.

Or am I imagining it? Did I really place it at the edge? Or was it the spine, or just think I did? Was I confused? Stop, Adam, you are becoming paranoid.

I don't like being confused. And with Hans's attack on me in my apartment and the violence in Mort's store, I was attracting too much attention that was reflecting badly on those I had become attached to. I feared not for myself, but for those I now called friends.

Not Born of Woman

I again made an entry in my journal, then opened the *Amuletae boni et mali*.

It was with that mindset I read more about the objects of power in the book and all the occult forces they claimed to harness.

That was the other factor—were the things spoken of in the treatise real or human misconstructions of objective phenomena? The essences I could see, the survival of the life energy of living things, were they the same as the ghosts spoken of in so many texts? And if they were real—at least in some form, as I knew them to be—were the demons oft writ of real as well? And what other folk horrors were real? Werewolves? Vampires? And other monsters—like me?

For what was I?

By the standards of many, I was a *mullo*, a revenant, or perhaps a zombie. The priest I had pledged to help would curse me if he knew my real nature. And would Mort be so friendly if he knew? I had been shunned as a monster after my creation, a victim of the same fears that Lovecraft spoke of.

Were my attempts to understand humans really worth it when I knew that most would deny my very existence or hate me for it out of hand?

Yet there was Vandoma. She was the first person to know who I am and not shy away in horror.

I tried to put it all out of my mind as I read the book and tried to place it in the puzzle of it all.

I took the precaution of locking my outer office door and bracing a chair against the inner one and read until I dozed in my chair, my dreams full of angular shapes and crimson shards.

CHAPTER EIGHTEEN

I woke to the sound of Vandoma's typewriter in the outer office. I was stiff from sleeping in my office chair so stretched and walked to the door to open it.

"Good morning, Miss Kalderash." I startled her, as I expect she had no idea I was in the office.

"Oh, Mister Paradise," she said. "I did not realize—"

"That's okay," I answered. "I don't usually sleep here." I must have looked worse than usual with my clothes rumpled and my hair a mess. I also realized I had not applied any makeup to minimize my facial scars, but none of this seemed to phase her.

"Would you like me to go downstairs to get you some coffee and breakfast?" she asked. She was already rising, and I suspected I would have to argue her out of going down.

"Thank you," I said. "Please get yourself some tea and breakfast as well—all on my tab, of course." She smiled at this.

I added, "I'll head to the washroom and freshen up." She went down the stairs while I visited the washroom where I put myself together and wet and combed my hair. By the time she came back up, I had changed into a spare suit in the office and felt presentable. I also felt comfortable enough with her to not apply my usual makeup.

"Is the sandwich as you wish?" she asked as we sat in her office and ate.

"It's fine," I replied. "Thank you again for going down for it."

Not Born of Woman

Today she was wearing a dark blue-grey dress and jacket. I thought she looked to have applied a little makeup as well, but I could have been mistaken.

"It was nothing, Mister Paradise," she said. "I was going to go for my own as well."

We ate in comfortable silence for a little bit then I asked, "Was there trouble with your brother last night when he came home after your mother found out about—"

Her face lit in a mischievous grin. "My mother was not happy," she said, "but he was even more unhappy when she talked to him about it."

"I am sorry that I made things—uncomfortable."

"No," she insisted, "it was Nico that was uncomfortable, but my mother made it clear to him that he was to help you undo what he had done. And … and if it is necessary that we speak to the police, then we will."

"I was going to ask you about that, Vandoma," I said. "I did not wish for—"

"No." She stopped me. "He yelled to Mother that 'I am man,' but she yelled back 'no man endangers his family's luck to bet on animals that are not even fit to pull a family wagon, only a boy does!' and so he will not be gambling again." She was positively gleeful, and I could see her brother must have ridden roughshod over her for years.

Good for you, Mother Kalderash.

"Nico will help you now," she continued. "All that you want."

"That will be a great help," I said, lowering my voice. "You have already been a great help …" I was trying to find a way to broach the subject of going to Tommy's but she was ahead of me again.

"Also, I am ready to go talk to the policemen," she said with a little pride in her tone. "The Kalderash family will do what is right."

"I don't doubt you will," I said. I told her I'd promised Tommy we'd visit that morning.

"I am ready," she said, rising. "Let us go."

I laughed. "Yes, Miss Kalderash, as you order, so we shall do!"

We caught a taxi and went directly to Tommy's precinct. I noticed that her determination faltered a bit as we approached the building, and she noticed all the blue uniforms who looked our way.

"Don't mind them looking at us," I said to ease her mind. "Even with my makeup added they are staring at me—they think I am some sort of thug come to start trouble."

"Why would they think that?"

I gave a gentle laugh. "Really? You don't think I look like a thug who starts barroom fights?" Her expression said it all—she really didn't. "You are kind, but really, it is not you they are looking at. They do not see you as a Roma; in this case, believe me, I am the object of their interest."

Once inside, the desk sergeant recognized me, and we were ushered into my friend's office.

"Adam," Tommy said, rising from his cluttered desk. "And—"

"Miss Vandoma Kalderash," I said. "This is Detective First Class Thomas Shane."

He held out his hand and she took it in a handshake.

"Thank you for coming in, Miss Kalderash," Tommy said. "We appreciate your help."

He indicated two chairs in front of his desk and we both sat. I presented him with the lists of pawnshops and explained what her brother and her tribe had found out so far.

"That's fantastic work, both of you," Tommy said as he went through the lists. "It would have taken my guys weeks to get this detailed a list of likely fences, let alone ones specifically looking out for these do-dads the Nazi boys seem to be looking for."

"Except, Tommy, I don't think the Nazis are the only ones looking for these objects."

"How so, Adam?"

"Well, when I had my little meeting with the Bundists the other night they were asking me where the *Koshti Bok* of the Kalderash family was. So, that tells me that even if Dorfman originally wanted it on behalf of the Nazis someone else has it now."

"The series killer?" Tommy said.

Not Born of Woman

"Yes," I agreed. "But how that intersects with the disappearances and deaths of these girls—that escapes me."

"Me as well," Tommy said. "But those symbols on the last girl—sorry to be so graphic, ma'am—I had one of our artists make a drawing of them from her and all the dead girls—it's accurate. Here they are." He held out a couple of pages that had the symbols on them from the dead girls, with notes as to the date each was found to provide a timeline. "I thought you would be better and faster finding out their meanings than we would, looking into those alchemists you talked about. It seems whoever our killer is, they have the same interest as the paperhanger's people."

"This thing they have done," Vandoma spoke up with only a little hesitation as she looked at the figures. "These evil signs they have made, you say they are associated with the *Koshti Bok*?" There was pain in her question.

"No," I hurried to say. "Your necklace does have an association with powers some might call occult, Vandoma, but as I showed you in the *Amuletae boni et mali* many objects have this. These deaths occurred before the necklace was pawned, so you must think of it as simply something else they wish to obtain, not at all the reason for the deaths."

She took my statement to heart, and I saw her tension ease.

"Miss Kalderash," Tommy added, "we in no way feel you are responsible for any of this, but we do think your contacts with your tribe can help us find this killer. What your brother has already done with these lists has cut out some of our work and we appreciate it."

She was clearly stunned to be treated so fairly. I realized as she relaxed how tense she had really been, holding herself with perfect control the whole time. She was a strong woman.

"The Kalderash will do all that we can to stop these terrible things," she said.

"And we will do what we can do to recover your necklace, miss," Tommy added in exchange. "We serve all the people of the city."

Good for you, Tommy. This was the reason he had become my friend.

"So, what's the next move?" I asked.

"If you would see what these symbols mean," he said, "and if Miss Kalderash can put out word to her people to keep looking for these sort of items—" He smiled. "I know for a fact that more people will be careless in conversation in front of 'regular' folks than with any of my investigators. I know we have not always seemed to be on your people's side, miss, but trust me, we are."

She acknowledged his kindness with a shy smile and a nod.

"Perhaps if my—" she began but a uniform pulled the door open and pushed his head in.

"Detective Shane," the cop said, out of breath. "We just got a 10-13 from that priest's place. O'Malley called and then the line went dead."

"Crud!" Tommy exclaimed. He ran to his coat rack and grabbed his overcoat and hat. "Sorry, I have to—"

"We're coming," I said in no uncertain terms. He only spared a second for a stern look then headed out the door. We followed.

"First time in the back of a police car?" I whispered to Vandoma as the squad car pulled away from the station.

"Yes," she whispered. She looked over at me and, as uncomfortable emotionally as she was, giggled at seeing me bent up to fit in the car.

"I know," I said, acknowledging my hunched-over position. "Not much seems built for me."

We rode the rest of the way in a tense silence except for the calls on the police radio that called for ambulances, more police, and to throw a cordon around the block on which the rectory was located. Tommy was clearly upset and murmured a prayer under his breath.

The car had barely skidded to a stop before Tommy jumped out to be met by a very upset uniformed officer.

"It's bad, Tommy," the officer said, not giving Vandoma and me a second glance. "O'Malley found them when he came to relieve Harris."

There were other uniforms around, some taking photographs and even dusting the door to the rectory that was ajar.

Just inside the door was the body of a large man in a brown suit lying face down on the floor with two bullet wounds in his back. There was a cardboard tray with what looked like soft drinks spilled and scattered near the body along with what looked to be butcher paper-wrapped sandwiches.

Above the body, the black and crimson essence of his existence spiraled up and hovered, attesting to the violence and suddenness of his death. It almost felt as if it was crying out to me for vengeance.

Tommy stopped for a moment, and I saw he was gathering himself for what was to come.

"Ah, Mikey," he muttered as he looked at the corpse.

"The others are upstairs," the uniformed officer said. Tommy went white.

"How many?" my friend asked.

"So far, three."

"Damn," Tommy said. He turned back to us. "Ma'am you have to stay down here. Come with me, Adam."

"I think it's for the best, Vandoma," I said. "I don't think it will be good to see what's up there."

"Yes," she said. She looked down at the body and muttered a prayer. "Be careful, Mister Paradise." She stayed at the door with one of the other uniforms who eyed her suspiciously.

"Lead us up, O'Malley, and fill us in," Tommy said. "And Dembrowski—" he said to the officer by Vandoma, "take care of the lady." His tone left no doubt that the patrolman was to be nice to the Roma woman.

Thanks, Tommy.

Officer O'Malley gave a running commentary.

"The way it looks, somebody came to the door with a food delivery," O'Malley said. "When Harris turned to lead them in, the killer shot Mike in the back." He led us through the wood-paneled corridor and up the stairs to where I knew Father Burton's study was located.

I felt a cold shiver of fear at what we were about to see; it seemed that the terror and death continued to multiply with each passing day.

When will it end?

CHAPTER NINETEEN

"The killer must have had a silencer," O'Malley continued as we reached the top of the stairs, "because they came up here as bold as you please and encountered the housekeeper right at the top."

When we reached the landing, we could see the body of the old woman who had been the housekeeper, lying on her back, eyes wide, frozen in the last moment of terror. The phantom of her spirit, an indigo cloud of what had been her, floated above the body.

There was a neat bullet hole directly in the center of her forehead.

"Jeeze," Tommy murmured.

"The others are down that way," O'Malley indicated where I knew the priest's office was. We moved forward with a growing sense of dread.

At the door of the office, we paused.

Inside was a scene of carnage and death.

A young boy in a school uniform from the nearby Catholic high school was slumped over the front of Father Burton's desk with several bloody holes in his back, his white shirt a blossom of red. His essence of a life barely lived was so small, just a faint swirl of indigo over his corpse.

"How the hell do you tell his parents?" Tommy whispered. I was aware that the boy could not be much older than his own son.

Father Burton's body was on the other side of the desk, collapsed in the corner below the window. His eyes were wide, his face twisted in a mask of pain that clearly told the story of his last moments of life.

Not Born of Woman

"This is sick," Tommy gasped. I thought my friend was going to be physically ill at the sight of the man he knew so well, now dead.

The body of the priest told the story of a killer filled with anger. There were bullet holes in each of his knees, his stomach, and one in his forehead. He had obviously been tortured with those shots to his body before the final headshot had ended his agony.

The phantom form that eddied and flowed over him was a jagged thing of black and indigo, shot with slashes of crimson. The gold that had glowed in his life of those souls linked to him was gone now, banished by the agonizing moments of his death.

"This is just horrible," Tommy said after he had caught his breath. Then he was all business. "I want all this dusted, photographed. Every hair, every fiber. Anything that could be a clue. And I want every son of a bitch who has ever had a parking ticket in this town grilled."

O'Malley nodded then whispered, "A priest, a kid, the old lady — and one of our own."

"I know," Tommy said, then spoke as if it was a prayer. "We'll get him."

I finally felt I could speak. "There will be no way to keep this from the papers; you're going to have to get ahead of it." He looked at me and blinked as if waking from a nightmare.

"Yes, Adam, you're right. Let's get out of here. I'll need to call the commissioner and the chief. They need to tell the mayor."

We retraced our steps downstairs and outside where we rejoined Vandoma. She saw our faces and put a hand on my arm.

"It is very bad, yes?" she said.

"Yes," I said in a somber tone. I could see in her expression that she understood the level of the horror of it all.

"How do you read it, Adam," Tommy asked me, I think more to reassure himself that he had accessed the situation correctly on his own than to really get my opinion. He was a very good cop, but that meant he was open to any source of information. I did not mind; I wanted to help in any way I could.

"Someone impersonated a delivery person," I said as we all walked away from the building a little way as more technicians and the coroner team entered. "And they must have been pretty convincing for your

Officer Harris to let them in, lock the door and then turn his back on them to lead them toward the stairs."

"Yes," Tommy said, "Mike was no slouch."

"And they must have used a silencer since they caught the housekeeper upstairs unawares. They then moved to Father Burton's office and caught the schoolboy—I assume—as he rose from the chair and killed him quickly with two shots."

"And then," Tommy said with more anger in his voice than I had ever heard, "he deliberately and methodically shot Father Burton in each knee, his stomach and then finally put him out of his misery with the headshot."

"And did it systematically and sadistically," I noted. "This has the earmarks of the kind of torture that Dorfman and the other pawnbroker suffered." Tommy nodded, obviously thinking the same thing.

"I've never seen anything so cold-blooded," O'Malley observed. His florid Irish face was splotched with whiteness as he too clearly fought being sick. He and Tommy were both devout Catholics and this went to the core of their lives, their worldview, and all they held dear.

I had, sadly, in my time among mankind, seen cruelty to match this but not recently. And not in a way that touched me so directly—I had promised both Tommy and, by implication, Guido Manzetti that I would safeguard the priest. I had failed miserably.

And more than that, it seemed certain the deaths were both related to the string of series killings of the girls and the *Koshti Bok* of the Kalderash family.

"This will blow up big, Adam," Tommy finally admitted. "I can't cut you or Miss Kalderash any slack on this now."

"You won't need to," I said. "I'll get on these symbols directly from here."

"And I shall have my brother and the tribe begin to look for any of these objects," Vandoma said, "as well as our *Koshti Bok*. This terrible thing—it affects us all."

Tommy heard the sincerity in her voice and acknowledged it with a faint smile. "Yes, it does, miss." He turned to me. "I have to get things going here."

Not Born of Woman

"And I have to get things going as well," I said. "I'll keep in close contact."

"I'll probably be sleeping at the precinct," he said. "It will be all hands on deck from this point out."

"You'll hear from me later," I said. "And don't let this shake your faith, Tommy."

"Take care," Tommy said with a nod that acknowledged my attempt at consolation. "This madman has gone over every line that ever was—there's no going back from this. No one is safe. Not even you, big guy, so watch yourself."

There was no time to be wasted so Vandoma and I took a taxicab directly from the murder scene to Digger's bookstore, even though I would have made the short walk if I had been alone.

"I have this and one other stop I should make before I return to the office," I said to her as we approached the store. "I hope you don't mind—they'll be brief."

"No, I do not, Mister Paradise," she said. "I know this is most important." There was a deep sadness in her tone, and I imagined I knew why—her family's luck was so irreparably tied to multiple deaths that she feared the reproach and shame this would bring on her people. The Roma had been blamed for other crimes with less connection than her necklace.

"This is none of your doing," I tried to reassure her again as we exited the cab. When she looked away from me, I said more stridently, "You must understand that. Whatever is motivating this killer, your connection to this affair—by your brother's unfortunate pawning of the *Koshti Bok*—comes well after the fact. These other killings happened before your necklace was involved and are not connected to your people. You saw that Tommy—Detective Shane—did not hold you or your tribe guilty."

"Always they find a way to blame the Roma." She was firmly convinced that history would repeat itself and I really could not give the guarantee that it would not.

"All I can say is, he's a fair man. And I will do all I can to see that no stain of this will mark the Kalderash or the Roma."

She gave me a gentle smile. "Yes, Mister Paradise, I know this is so. I will try to have faith as my mother said. You are *pajivalo Martja*, an honorable spirit of the dead. And you are my friend."

"Yes, Vandoma," I said. "Above all, I am your friend."

"'Better to illuminate than merely to shine ....'" Digger began as I entered, his voice trailing off when he saw Vandoma.

I finished the phrase with, "'... to deliver to others contemplated truths than merely to contemplate.' Thomas Aquinas. That was easy." I saw he was speechless for once as he looked at my companion.

"Digger Tome," I said, "may I introduce Miss Vandoma Kalderash."

After a moment when he blinked like an owl, he surprised me and said in Romani, "Lachi tiri dives."

"And good day to you," she replied in Romani before she realized he had spoken her language.

For a moment even I was taken aback. He saw this and grinned. "I'm not just a *helluo libertas*, you know."

"I never called you just a bookworm, my friend," I said. "But that is what I must call upon now." I produced the papers that Tommy had copied from the dead girls.

He took it from me, squinted his eyes, and stared at them with great concentration. While he did, Vandoma moved along the stacks of books with great fascination and, I suspect, to give us a modicum of privacy.

"Is this connected to the uh ... delicate matter you brought me the other day?" He lowered his voice and glanced at Vandoma.

"Yes," I whispered. "And it is connected to the deaths of the young girls." He pushed the glasses up his nose with a finger and made an "O" with his mouth.

"I'm afraid I can't say more, but these symbols have a greater importance because of ... other events that have occurred since then."

Not Born of Woman

He studied them intensely. "They are ancient, for certain," he said distractedly. "Possibly Sumerian or Babylonian. And some look to be Sanskrit. Hmmm." Then he looked up at me. "I will look at some books; it will take some time."

"It is time-sensitive," I said. "I am sorry to press—"

"I have a vague idea what this is about," he said with a tone that implied that indeed he might. "Can you come by tomorrow? Or maybe even tonight?"

"I'll stop by before dinner time," I said thankfully. "I'll buy the feast regardless."

"I would like to purchase this book," Vandoma held up a book of the French poetess Amable Tastu's verses.

"You are the first person to pick up that book of the estimable Eighteenth-Century French lady since I have had it in my store, dear Miss Kalderash," he said with a wide smile. "You are welcome to it with my blessings."

"Oh, no," she said. "I could not—"

"Yes, you can," he interrupted her. "Saint Thomas Aquinas also said, 'Man cannot live without joy; therefore, when he is deprived of true spiritual joys it is necessary that he become addicted to carnal pleasures.' I would not deprive you of that spiritual surcease. Books are a pleasure meant to be read and appreciated. Give me this carnal pleasure to share it with you."

She could not argue with so eloquent a gift and she acquiesced to his request. She bowed her head in surrender. "Thank you, sir."

"I'll see you later, Digger. Thank you," I said as we left.

"Later," he said, and he added with more life than I had heard from him in a while, "and come by any time, miss."

Once we were outside, she looked up at me with wonder. "He did not look at me as—as—"

"As Roma, or as broken?" I finished. She nodded. "No, he did not. He does not see only my appearance, either. He values what is within."

"Yes." She truly seemed confused by the vision of the non-Romani world she'd had that day. It was a new way of seeing for her. "As do you, Adam Paradise. I say again, you are a most unusual person."

"As are you, Vandoma Kalderash. Now, I have to grab another cab for a quick stop at my apartment. I want to get a change of clothing—I suspect I will be living out of the office for the foreseeable future."

CHAPTER TWENTY

When we arrived at my building, Dottie was sitting on the stoop of their apartment taking advantage of a bright, sunny day. They waved to me, arching an eyebrow when they saw Vandoma exit the cab behind me. I waved back and called, "I'll stop by on the way out."

"There were a couple of unpleasant types prowling around last night," Dottie said.

"Oh?"

"I think they were looking for you, Adam. They watched your apartment from across the street for a bit, but never crossed over."

"Thanks," I said.

Vandoma decided to accompany me up to my place where I paused at the door and crouched to look at the doorjamb.

"What do you do?" she asked.

"I had some problem with … uh … two-legged vermin," I said, "so I don't want to be surprised again. I took a hair and wet it and applied it to the door bridging to the jam. It is still here. Had it not been …."

She understood and nodded.

I stood, unlocked the door, and gestured. "Miss Kalderash, welcome to my very humble home."

She entered, clutching her new poetry book to her chest, and looked around my studio. It was simple to be sure, sparse in many ways with only one painting of Notre Dame Cathedral on the wall by the door, a bookcase overflowing with volumes, a single chair near an upright reading lamp, and the roughly made bed.

I had a small hot plate near the sink by the water closet and an armoire that served as my only closet. I went to it and removed a change of clothes.

While I gathered my things, Vandoma looked at my bookcase and then out the window to the panorama of the city and the Empire State Building that was the chief and best feature of this former artist's studio.

"It is truly an amazing thing that such a building was made by man," she said. She looked back at me as I finished filling a valise. "This is a strange city, a place of so many contrasts."

"Yes, it is," I said. "Mankind is so wide a canvas for the creator to paint his pictures."

She looked at me with questioning eyes when I said that.

Does she realize I look at that canvas from outside? Yes, now she must and yet it does not seem to frighten her.

We left the room, and I relocked it, putting my follicle security in place before we went down the stairs.

"I have not seen you around, Adam," Dottie asked me when we exited. "How is the leg and who is this charming creature?" They were in full makeup in a blue skirt suit with a pink shawl around their shoulders.

It was not until we got close that Vandoma realized how unique Dottie was. To her credit she was only surprised and not shocked.

"Dottie," I said, "this is Vandoma Kalderash. I am doing some investigating for her. And my leg is fine."

"Glad to meet you, dear," Dottie said. After a moment, the Roma woman smiled and held out her hand for Dottie to shake. "This hunk Adam doesn't bring guests around very much."

"It is very nice to meet you, Dottie," Vandoma said. "Have you known Mister Paradise long?"

Dottie looked at me with a sly smile before they answered. "Not deep nor long enough, dearie." Then they both laughed.

"Incorrigible," I sighed. Then I got serious. "What did the ones you saw hanging around look like?"

"Rough customers," Dottie said. "Two of them; big brutes in cheap suits. Dark hair, Italian I would guess." They made a disgusted face that reflected a dark memory. "The kind that like to claim they are all men and are afraid they really are not."

"Thanks, Dottie," I said. "I'm afraid I've attracted a lot of unwanted attention of late so I'm staying at my office for the next couple of days. Keep an eye out in any case. I don't want any of the spillover from my life to make things difficult for you. Stay clear of any new faces and be careful."

"I've been avoiding those sorts all my life, Adam," they said. "But thanks. You take care of yourself; they were here because of you — my suitors dress better." They grinned at us.

"Nice to meet you, miss," Dottie said.

"And you," she said.

"Come, Vandoma, we will walk to Fourteenth Street to catch another taxi."

"Stop by anytime," Dottie said. "I'm here most of the time; I do languid well. Take care, Adam."

I waved back and the Roma and I walked up to Fourteenth Street and Eighth Avenue.

"Your friend—" she began.

"Dottie?"

"Yes," she said. "He ... uh ... she, is like that all the time?" She was trying hard not to offend but her confusion was clear.

"Whenever they can be," I said. "At other times they are Daniel. It isn't safe for them to be their true self all the time, or in very many places."

She considered this for a few moments then said, "Yes, this I understand." And I was sure she did.

Back at my office, after ordering lunch from Mort, we both went to our separate tasks, me to research the symbols in the books I had there and she to finish the manuscript she was typing for *Weirdmask Magazine*. I took a few moments to update my journal, to keep from getting frustrated when contemplating the symbols challenged my knowledge.

Jake brought up the tray with soft drinks and sandwiches for us along with the usual lunchtime newspapers.

"This is something, eh, Mister P," the freckled-faced teen said. "They say there's a regular mad killer loose in the city." The late morning editions already had the lurid details of the four murders at the rectory, though they had not yet connected them to the murders of the two pawnbrokers. It seemed only a matter of time until some reporter would make the connection.

"Just sensationalism, Jake," I said, attempting to downplay the story. I could see the subject upset Vandoma. "I'm sure most of it is made up."

"Sure seems amazing," he said. "They said here the guy was a saderist."

"You mean sadist," I corrected.

"Golly, I guess so," he said. Then he shrugged. "What does the word sadist mean?"

"It means someone who takes delight in hurting other people, Jake."

"Wow, why?" he said, eyes bulging. He blanched, crossed himself, and muttered a silent prayer. "That's not right."

"No," I said. "Sometimes people are hurt and lash out by hurting others. Then again, sometimes there is no discernable reason that causes people to lack empathy and wish to hurt others and do it for enjoyment. The sadist can express themselves in many forms: as men who use women, bullies, and even some who hide their true nature and appear to be pillars of the community. Their love for cruelty, knowing they have caused suffering to others, is what gives them pleasure."

"Geeze Louise, Mister P," the boy said with awe and a shiver I took to show his disturbance. "That just don't sound right."

I tried to lighten the mood. "No, it is not right, I'm afraid, Jake, but there is a lot not right with the world; all we can do is try to be as right as we can."

"And have faith that good will win in the end," Vandoma added. She looked at me and smiled and I found myself wanting to believe her words but with all I had seen in my time back in civilization, I was skeptical.

Then there was my own behavior—was I the bully with the Bundists? Surely, I did not derive actual pleasure from hurting Hans, but I felt no particular guilt from it either. As always, I examined my motives and compared them to those of the ones around me. Looking at Vandoma and listening to her words did give me hope and all I could do was try to do good, deed by deed, and as she said, "hope for the best."

"Sure makes me a bit scared to go out there in the city," Jake said as he headed through the door. "Between them ratzies last week and this Jack the Ripper guy, makes me want to carry a baseball bat around with me."

"Or a bottle of seltzer?" I offered and got a shy smile from him.

When he'd left Vandoma looked at me. "You frightened the boy."

"I didn't mean to; sometimes I forget how young people are." When I realized what I had said, I added, "I meant that he is only a teenager."

"No," she said, "you meant what you said." Her eyes focused intently on me. "I know you are unlike any I have ever met; the stories of my people, they are of another time. You are of another time as well, are you not?"

"Yes," I said. I sat on a second chair in her office, opposite the desk she was using. "I am of another time, or perhaps of no time at all, I don't really know anymore."

"Where did you come from?" She was bold in asking and I could see she had wanted to ask since last night when her mother told her of my origin.

"Honestly, I know not; no more than any man may say they were born of their parents." She did not believe me so I continued, "I knew only my 'father' if you will—who wrested me from the dust of the earth, remnants of the discarded and dead. Where I was 'before' the moment I opened my eyes as you see me now, I do not know. Nor do I know where I shall go when my eyes close for the last time."

The enormity of the statement seemed to strike her then and I saw her draw back within herself for a moment, but then she seemed to accept it. "It does not matter; you are a good man," she said, emphasizing the word *man*, "and I believe what I have seen in your hand and what my mother saw. That you are here is the work of Providence, you are a *pajivalo Martja*, this I know."

I had not told the Roma woman a lie, but only the truth as far as I could express it. It was true that when I opened my eyes on the table in my creator Victor's laboratory, I was as I am, but that was not my first awareness; no, that was a vast grey time, a proto consciousness that had no formed thoughts but was definitely there.

In that greyness, after a time there was sound: a low, dull quick sound such as a watch wrapped in cotton might make. In that timeless time, I had flashes of things—a hand holding a cup, a foot in a stirrup, a flash of lightning illuminating a face beside me in a bed—though I did not know until much later what they were.

I had already endured the cold of the arctic for many years when the Shelly woman fictionalized my tale, yet that literary moment of creation might well have been my real awakening, for when I returned from the icy wastes, I had learned I was already a legend of the Roma. And I was part of the mythology of the west.

During that long sojourn of isolation, I experienced other flashes, moments of memory if you will, in my body. They were the sensation in one hand of holding the hand of another that was of similar color. There was the feel of phantom sunshine on my neck, the smell of flowers or perfume from some other life. I experienced feelings from nerve endings as if someone was pressed against me, and even the minutiae of sensation as if someone was breathing on my cheek.

Memories trapped in my flesh? Shadows of the lives that each part of me had lived, or something else?

Buddhists and some Christian sects believed in reincarnation, that the essence of an individual continues, and I knew that the shapes and amorphous forms I saw each day were the remnant energy of living, conscious beings that survived after death. I saw those shapes hover and swirl around me all the time, different and distinct for each arm, for my one leg, and other more nonspecific phantoms. They were so constant I was barely conscious of them.

Even my very brain had a "life" before my current consciousness, but those moments of existence seemed beyond me—perhaps its former 'occupant' had moved on where the circumstances of the rest of me—of my parts—were more blurred and their fates unclear.

All of it was a constant source of exploration for me as it had been for so many years. What was I and who was I? Where did I fit into the scheme of the cosmic puzzle?

None of this could really be formed into a coherent phrase I could express, at least not simply to the woman before me. Instead, I said, "'We are not human beings having a spiritual experience,'" quoting Teilhard de Chardin, "'We are spiritual beings having a human experience.' I am working to have a truly human experience and I thank you for helping me in this."

She took the words to heart and accepted them. I felt honored that she did.

"I must finish this typing," she said, putting our discussion to an end, "then I can call my home to talk to my brother and find out what more the tribe has discovered."

"And I should get to my notes on the symbols. I want to get a map of the city and plot out a route to visit as many of the pawnshops your brother found were dealing with artifacts before I go to visit Digger later."

"It is good that you spoke such to me, Mister Paradise," she said looking up from where she was shuffling papers in preparation to resume her work. "We should be honest."

After so many years where I could not share my truth with anyone, where I was locked, as it were, in my own mind and could only see myself in the echoes of my own thoughts—here was a person who knew and did not see me as a demon. It was almost as shocking to me as my revelation must have been to her.

"Yes, Vandoma," I said. "It is. Honesty and truth are powerful allies in the pursuit of good."

CHAPTER TWENTY-ONE

By lunchtime, Vandoma had finished her typing and I had been able to find several of the symbols in my reference books. I did not like what I found. All the symbols I identified were associated with dark forces and were symbols of power. I was sure that Digger would have even better luck though I feared what he would find.

I had also mapped out the easiest way to get to all the targeted pawnshops to look for other leads to the killer who was so interested in the occult. I closed the *Amuletae boni et mali* and stepped into the outer office as Vandoma was packing up her work.

"Good timing," I said. "I thought we should go and get some lunch at a diner near here and then send you home in a cab while I go prowling the pawnshops."

She considered for a moment. "I will have lunch, but then I will take the train home. You cannot continue to spend money on taxicabs. It is wasteful." I could see her mind was set.

"As you wish, Miss Kalderash," I said as she started to close her typewriter. "You are taking it with you?"

"I thought I would be a distraction with all you must do," she said.

"Not at all," I said, perhaps a bit too quickly. "It will be good to have you here to coordinate with your brother and the police while I run around."

She paused, looking down at her typewriter, then her face brightened when she looked up. "I do have other work—such silly writing is made in large numbers for these pulp magazines."

Not Born of Woman

"Good, it is settled then. You can start thinking about what you want for lunch while I grab my hat and coat." When we left the office, I performed my hair across-the-doorjamb-security exercise again. With all the ambushes of late it would do to take precautions.

We went downstairs to the drug store where Vandoma called her house to see if her brother had any news for her while I spoke with Mort.

"I'm going to be out for the rest of the afternoon," I said to the genial old man while he straightened some packages of candy on the counter. "So, if anyone calls just take a message. I should be back before you close up, but if not, just leave them in the foyer—no need to go upstairs to my office."

"You're so busy," he said with a chuckle as he cast a glance toward the phone booths. "Since the nice lady came by."

"Yes," I acknowledged, "things have gotten busy, to say the least. I'm afraid I will have to put off our Hebrew lessons for a little bit."

He made a tsking sound. "One should never put off learning, Adam."

"I know, Mort," I answered, "but I'm deep in a case that requires a lot of focus."

He lowered his voice, "Does it have to do with those *meshugas* that were in here yesterday?"

"Yes, if only tangentially," I said. "I wish I could tell you more, but ...."

"I understand," he said. "But let me give you some advice, my friend—take some time for yourself. It is not good to work all the time." His face darkened and he was lost in thought. "The world is becoming a dark place, Adam. With the National Socialists Party, it is even darker now. After last November ...."

I saw in his eyes that he was in deep pain. "The night of broken glass?" He looked at me with surprise. While many Americans had ignored the news reports, I had read of the horror in Germany three months before. The brown-shirted legions of Nazis thugs had rampaged in one night across synagogues and Jewish stores across the country, smashing windows, desecrating holy sites, and attacking and killing Jews. At least ninety were murdered outright. The German authorities stood by and did nothing.

"Yes, the Krystallnacht," he said with agony barely contained. "The Nazi Sturmabteilung burned and smashed synagogues, killed my people in a pogrom like in Prague, like in Russia—like so often in history. My people always crushed beneath the heels of oppressors. Bullies, thugs; monsters."

I put a hand on his arm. "I know, my friend. The world has treated your people so poorly for so long."

"And what do we have to fight back with? Learning? How can learning alone match the brutes of the world?"

"You have your faith."

"Faith?" His laugh was bitter. "Yes, a faith that has endured even after the fall of the Temple, the Diaspora, and now this—how much can faith alone sustain a people? Sometimes it is not enough to endure, Adam. The *Maccabeus* knew this. Rabbi Judah Loew ben Bezalel of Prague knew this. Sometimes one must take up the jawbone of the ass to oppose the oppressors."

"You are not a man of violence," I said.

"True." He shrugged as if to banish the dark mood and worked to smile. "But the Talmud says, 'A person will be called to account on Judgment Day for every permissible thing he might have enjoyed but did not.' Perhaps sometime, I will get to fight back for my people. In the meantime, I have Jake to break bottles over the bully boy's heads when they bother me, yes?"

"And me," I said. "And a lot of other good people who will help."

"Yes, you are a good man, Adam." He smiled and was his jovial self again. "Do not let an old man's aches and pains bother you. Young people like you should be thinking of good things." He glanced at Vandoma who was walking toward us from the phone booths and added with mischief, "She is a nice girl, I can tell."

Before I could respond, the Roma woman spoke. "My mother says Nico and her argued last night, then he left and did not return home. She is worried and so am I."

"It's good we forego lunch, and you head home then," I said. "And no argument about me putting you in a taxicab. I will call you at home if anything develops here." I looked over to Mort. "If her brother comes by looking for her—"

"I will tell the boy to call her at home," he said. He gave her a genuine smile. "I am sure he will be all right, miss."

"Thank you."

We started to head out and Mort handed her a peppermint candy. She took it and gave a girlish giggle.

To me he also quoted the Talmud, "'Never expose yourself unnecessarily to danger, a miracle may not save you ... and if it does, it will be deducted from your share of luck or merit.'"

"Yes, Papa Gluckman," I said, "I will take care."

I brooked no objection from Vandoma and sent her home to her mother in a cab with a promise to call in an hour or so to see how she was.

I watched the taxi pull away from the curb with discomfort at seeing her go.

Absurd to manufacture worry. She will be fine and I am sure Nico can take care of himself. Still, I felt uneasy as I walked to the diner to get a meal. I expected to be traveling the rest of the day as I attempted to find some clue to where the *Koshti Bok* was and who had perpetrated all the killings. And why.

I was almost to the diner when a dark sedan pulled up to the curb beside me. A dark-haired man slid smoothly out of the open door to step in front of me. He opened his overcoat to let me see a shoulder holster.

"Mister Manzetti wants to see you," he said. His attempt to menace me was somewhat undercut by the fact that he barely came to my shoulder in height. He was well within the sweep of my arms, and I could have stopped him from reaching his weapon if I wanted to but there seemed no point. I had planned to visit the loan shark again sometime that day anyway.

I squeezed into the back seat and the gunman joined me, looking even smaller sitting at my side. He had a thin, pencil mustache and dead eyes that he focused on me.

The diver needed no instruction and pulled into traffic.

At least he didn't feel the need to send a team after me. I can only assume Manzetti knew I would not make a fuss—clearly this was a "soft" invitation.

We rode in silence through midday traffic.

To my surprise, we did not go to the café where Manzetti usually held court, but to a side street underneath the Brooklyn Bridge in Chinatown. We stopped at a warehouse built into the stone arched base of the bridge. My gunman escort stepped out and waited while I unfolded myself from the car, then indicated the door of the warehouse with a point of his chin.

There was another armed thug in an ill-fitting overcoat standing by the door and he opened it for me.

Inside was a cavernous space. From the empty and cobweb-covered vats and other machinery, the detritus of boxes, and the inevitable broken furniture scattered about, it looked to have been an illegal brewery before repeal.

A third gunman, this one in a bright blue suit, met me inside and led me through a corridor of crates between the vats to a cleared space in the back where Guido "Tony" Manzetti was seated behind a desk.

There were two silent types on either side of him with hands resting under their suit jackets.

"Mister Paradise," Manzetti said.

"Mister Manzetti," I replied. There was a chair in front of his desk, and I sat without invitation, hopeful that the aged wood would not break beneath my weight.

We sat in uneasy quiet for a few moments, then the gang boss pulled up the fixings of a cigarette, rolled it, and waited while one of his guards stepped up to light it for him.

"The priest—" he began as he blew out some smoke.

"I know," I interrupted. "And the police officer guarding him as well as two others."

"It's not good." His statement was flat, almost abstract as if saying "the sky is blue."

Not Born of Woman

"No," I commented. "It is very, very bad. And unexpected."

"Not so unexpected if there was a cop there."

"No, true," I said. "But it was a very professional job—except it was also very much a crime of passion."

"Passion?" He said flatly again as if he did not understand that passion could exist.

"Father Burton was murdered in such a way that he was tortured—slow death. Somebody wanted him to suffer."

"Christ," he said with a sharp, clipped tone. He stubbed out the freshly lit cigarette in a glass ashtray on the desk. "You on this?" It was not really a question, more confirming an order.

"What I was doing today," I said. I saw no reason to hide anything from him. "I know for sure now that the person who killed the pawn dealers, those who kidnapped and murdered the girls that they've found, and killed the priest are the same person or persons."

He stared at me without any change in expression then nodded in sign to his guards. Both of them went off to the side, disappearing into the darkness between two vats.

We sat in silence with the smoke from the dying cigarette forming a curtain between us.

The scuffle of feet from the vats announced the return of the goons but this time with a limp figure between them: Nico.

"This Gypsy loser came to me last night in the middle of the night," Manzetti said. "Demanding—*demanding*—I get his dingus back for him. Tells me he's gonna put a freakin' hex on me for sellin' it." The loan shark did not raise his voice but was clearly very upset.

Nico looked to have been roughly handled, his right eye swollen, his lip bloody. The two guards just let go of the Roma and he dropped semi-conscious to the ground.

"Stay down," I said in Hungarian to him. "Let me handle this."

He looked up at me and for a moment he did not register it was me, but when he did, he seemed about to say something but fortunately stopped himself.

"You know this piece of waste?" Manzetti said with the same flat tone that he had most of the time.

"Tangentially," I said. "And I can tell you he is not who we are looking for, but he is the reason I got into this. I guess you can see this since you yourself gave him an alibis for the priest."

"You taking responsibility for this?"

"Yes," I said. "I can tell you that he probably came here because his mother read him the riot act last night and he felt bad for messing up and losing the necklace in the first place."

This made Manzetti break character and almost snort laugh. "You're okay, Paradise."

He leaned forward and his voice lowered to a dark whisper, "But this skell who killed the priest; I want him. Not the police, not you. I want him. Find him."

"I will do what I can to find him, Mister Manzetti and I have no particular interest in the official concept of justice. I will see you know what I know when I know it."

"Okay, good enough," Manzetti said. "Now get this Gypsy mess out of my sight—and make sure I don't ever see it again."

CHAPTER TWENTY-TWO

Manzetti's goons were kind enough to carry Nico outside the warehouse where they deposited him on the cold sidewalk and then went back inside. There was no mention of giving me or the Roma a ride.

"You did not have to talk to them about my mother," Nico said when he could get to his feet. He looked at me with considerable distaste.

"It amused him," I said. "That's probably the reason you're still alive. You have to understand human lives mean little to men like Guido."

"You mean Gypsy lives," he spat bitterly.

"Any lives," I said. "His sort view only family as worth anything."

"He seemed to treat you well enough."

I allowed myself to smile. "Respect is not the same as affection, Mister Kalderash. He would have no compunction about killing me if it suited him, but he knows mine is not a life to be taken easily. Predators like him respect one equation: is the effort worth the reward? The cost to kill me would be high, too high to justify it, and he knows it."

We walked a short distance into the busy lunchtime crowds of Chinatown with him gradually growing steadier on his feet.

Outside of a basement restaurant on Mott Street, I stopped him. "I'm hungry," I said. "I imagine you must be as well." He looked at the sign and the steps going down and made an unpleasant face.

"Here?"

"It opened last year," I said. "Wo Hop is family owned and they serve big portions."

"But—Chinese food?"

"Don't tell me you're prejudiced, Nico. Trying new things will do you good." He looked like he was going to argue with me, but I suspect he felt some sense of debt to me for extricating him from the mob boss, so he acquiesced and preceded me down the narrow stairs. I knew he looked in bad shape and didn't smell so fresh, but it was crowded, and the smells of the cooked food would keep attention from both of his faults. Besides, my size would draw most of the attention.

Inside was a crowded, cave-like basement, packed with customers, mostly Chinese but with a few hearty occidentals who had heard about the place. The waiter remembered me and that I left a good tip—as if he could forget me—so was able to find us seats in the corner after rearranging some tables.

"I do not know what to order," Nico said. His confusion was almost humorous.

"I'll order something for us both," I said. "They bring communal plates. So you'll be able to sample." As we had to raise our voices to be heard in the noisy restaurant, we both spoke in Romani which reduced any chance of being understood if overheard.

I was able to order in both English and halting Cantonese—I had been trying to learn some from a friend—and the waiter raced off.

The Roma seemed suddenly not so sure about coming into the space with me and looked around uncomfortably.

"What did you think you could do by going to Manzetti last night?" I asked him. His glare was an angry one, but he tempered his words.

"After you convinced my mother you were something special," he said with undisguised contempt, "I had to do something. None of my tribe have been able to find anything about these occult objects you wanted. I did not trust that gangster to have told me the truth ... I thought ... I thought he still had it."

"I admit it is possible he lied to you," I said. "He lies with considerable skill, but I see no profit for him to do so and profit is his main reason to be. It is the reason he wants the killer caught, ultimately; the police heat is bad for his business. And I suppose some part of him remembers a childhood of Sundays in church, so it will allow him to feel virtuous if he can say he stopped the killer."

The plates of food came then, and Nico looked at them with some concern.

"This is wonton soup. These are called chop suey," I said. "They're a mixture of bean sprouts, onions, celery, Chinese vegetables, and some meat. This is chicken chop suey, and this is pork chop suey."

He poked at them with a fork.

"This is chow mien," I added. I used a fork as well, as my hands were a bit too clumsy for chopsticks. "You can mix any of it with the white rice."

He screwed up his courage and sampled some of each of the dishes, tentatively at first but then with some gusto.

"See," I said, "you just had to give it a chance. Hunger always wins over fear."

I could see the Roma wanted to be angry at me but was too hungry to stop eating. As that hunger was sated, he slowed down and eventually was able to speak to me again.

"Why are you helping my sister?"

"I told you; she asked me. We made an agreement—for a good Roma meal."

He stared at me in disbelief. "No one does this—risks this—for just a meal."

I could not argue deeply with him; many might not risk what I had for such an apparently trifling price. But I would. At least at the beginning. Now, I was not so sure. There was so much more in the balance—my word to her, to Manzetti, to Tommy, and to myself.

I finally was able to quote St. Aquinas, "'There is nothing on this earth more to be prized than true friendship.' Your sister is my friend. I hope that you will be mine as well."

Nico was a little stunned by what I laid before him, a chance to save face and move forward with no prejudice for past attitudes. I believe that it's always the best path to keep the ego from interfering with positive interaction.

As we concluded our meal, the Roma seemed to have made his decision. Once I paid the bill and we were climbing up the steep steps from the basement restaurant he said, almost formally, "I thank you for your intervention, Mister Adam Paradise."

"It was and is my pleasure, Mister Nico Kalderash," I replied as formally. "I think you should call to relieve your mother and sister's concern, and then, perhaps head home."

He took this as good advice, and we went to a phone booth in an arcade on a nearby street. I allowed him his privacy for the call that, from the tone that made it through the glass of the door, sounded contrite.

When he came out of the booth he said, "I will go home."

"Allow me to pay for a taxi, Nico," I offered, "As a favor to your mother, not to you. Friend to friend."

He accepted this gesture, and we hailed a cab.

"I'll ride up to Twenty-Third Street,' I said. "I have a stop up there."

"It is not easy for one to sit and do nothing," the Roma admitted as we rode. "A man must act."

"Yes," I agreed, "and we are acting—but there is a time to gather oneself—to know the enemy, to know the land. Then is the time for action."

He nodded his head reluctantly. "As you say."

"We will make everything right again," I said. "Together."

He accepted my peace offering. We shook hands as I got out, and he went off in the cab to his family home.

I decided not to hit the pawnshops but to walk the short distance to Digger's bookstore in hopes he had some information ready for me. I admit I felt the need for speed in bringing some news to Tommy for I had a feeling that things were accelerating toward some dark destination.

"'Just as the soul fills the body, so God fills the world,'" Digger said as I entered. "'Just as the soul bears the body, so God endures the world.'" He grinned, thinking he had stumped me with our game, but I had been at my Hebrew studies even though I had not had my more advanced courses with Mort.

"By Orchot Tzadikim," I shot back with a laugh. "But you didn't finish it: 'Just as the soul sees but is not seen, so God sees but is not seen.'"

Not Born of Woman

Digger's expression showed shock for a second then he laughed a deep belly laugh. "I thought for sure this time." He had to stop for a moment to make change for a customer who bought a stack of old *Scientific American* magazines and then looked to me again. "But then I should know better, Adam," he finished.

"You'll stump me one of these days," I said, "If I don't stay sharp. One has to have a challenge to give purpose." I produced a pastrami sandwich I'd picked up on the way as partial payment for his research for me. He took it gratefully with a wide smile and inhaled it as if it was incense.

"Ah, you know me well, Adam," Digger said. Then his expression sobered. "Indeed, it was quite a challenge you set me with those symbols; you knew I would dive into them immediately."

"So, you were able to find out their meaning?"

"Yes." He looked up as the last customer wandered out of the store and waited until we were alone before he continued. "This is some very awesome stuff, Adam, in the old sense of the word." His tone was very serious. "I had to dig deep for it."

"Why so mysterious?" I had never heard him sound worried about anything before but there was darkness in his eyes.

"The symbols were from several civilizations, Adam. Hebrew, Sanskrit, Sumerian, Aramaic, even Coptic."

"I recognized the Hebrew, of course," I said, "and suspected the Sumerian. What did they say? Or mean?"

"They all seemed to be connected to one thing," he said. "You know the word golem, do you not?"

I did. A creature formed of the dust of the Earth and of clay that the bible called "Golmi"—an unfinished being before God's eyes. I had often pondered where I stood in relation to such a being. What difference to be composed of dead flesh than of dirt and mud? The first Adam of the Bible was initially created as a golem when his dust was "kneaded into a shapeless husk."

"Yes," I said. "But that is a concept of the Biblical tradition."

"Well, yes," he said, "But not strictly. The Qur'ran says that Allah created man from clay. Sumerian mythology says Enki and Ninmah created a servant of the gods out of the clay of the Abzu, the fresh water of the underground. The Egyptians say that Khnum created clay children to place in their mother's womb. And of course, there is the famous story of the Jewish golem of Prague created to fight oppression and so on with other religions as well."

"And that is what these symbols were about?"

"Yes," he said. "In each language represented it talks about creating life from clay—the typical Golem image. The Sumerian symbols talk about how Enkidu is created by the Goddess Aruru out of clay to be a companion to Gilgamesh." I saw his mind wander off as he started to recall some passage from the epic of Gilgamesh. "That Sumerian hero even eventually becomes fearful of his own death and decides to seek Utnapishtim, the Faraway, and learn the secret of eternal life. Utnapishtim and his wife are the only humans to have been granted immortality by the gods after the great flood in the story."

"But back to these symbols." I called him back from his reverie. "Are they all on the same subject?"

"Yes," he said. "I really didn't think so many cultures had similar tales to the golem, you know? But then I started to dig, and they all do. And all of them speak in some document or other of using objects of power to copy this concept of creating servant life from dirt, mud, or clay. It means any of those objects in the *Amuletae boni et mali* could be linked to this."

"The question is why?" I asked. "Why would this killer be obsessed with this particular myth?" Though I had a chilling premonition of what he was going to say.

His voice dropped to almost a whisper. "It was like someone was using summoning spells from many traditions to find a way to bring some hideous undead thing to life. Some of the myths speak of a blood price to bring that life. I think it is possible that these girls you told me about were murdered as sacrifices to some ancient gods!"

CHAPTER TWENTY-THREE

I promised to let Digger know how things progressed and walked over to the precinct where Tommy had his office. On the way, I picked up an afternoon edition of the *Daily Star* and discovered that the paper had more details of Father Burton's murder.

Can't keep it secret. Not something this horrible.

The reporter on the story was beginning to connect it to the series killings of the girls. Not directly yet, but there were implications in the story along with an editorial on the front page decrying the "new lawlessness that was sweeping the city," with callbacks to the Nazi rally. They had no idea how much relevance that statement had.

At the precinct, there was a distinct air of sadness and anger; the front of the building bore black bunting for the murdered officer. All the uniforms moving in and out of the building wore black armbands and grim expressions.

"It makes me sick," Tommy said when I entered his office. He was just hanging up the phone and when he looked up to see me, he looked ten years older than when I had seen him last. "Damn politicians see everything in terms of 'how will this affect my popularity'!"

"The mayor?" I asked.

"No, thank God," he said as he motioned me to sit across from him. "He's said we can have any resource we need. No, a state senator who is trying to figure out how to get in on this to boost his ratings with the public. Steams me up." He sat back in the chair and squeezed his eyes together and rubbed his temples.

"Headache?" I asked.

"Only beginning," he said. "I suspect it will get worse." He took a deep breath and tried to shake it off and asked, hopefully, "What are you doing here? I didn't think I'd see you 'til tonight."

I told him of my little talk with Manzetti.

"That complicates things," he said when I finished. "Vigilante justice is never pretty, though I swear I'd take any help on this, even thugs like Manzetti."

"Well, I don't think he will have any more luck with his methods," I said. "But I did have a little with these symbols." This got his attention, and he leaned forward.

"What are they?"

"Bear with me on this, Tommy, but remember I'm just the messenger." I told him what Digger had discovered about the symbols and his conjecture about why.

"So, some guy is killing these girls to make a voodoo monster?" he said. "That's nuts."

"I didn't say it was rational," I said. "And technically, a different thing than voodoo."

He didn't appreciate the humor.

"All I need is some kind of religious killer—" He seemed exhausted, and I knew it was because he took the safety of the city very personally. "Lust, hate, revenge, I can understand, but things like that …."

"Religious violence has been the worse kind in the history of mankind, my friend," I said. "People convinced their 'god' blesses them and excuses them for atrocities has predicated crusades, pogroms, and inquisitions since Babylon."

"This is 1939, Adam, that kind of medieval thinking—"

"'You think that a wall as solid as the earth separates civilization from barbarism. I tell you the division is a thread, a sheet of glass.'" He looked at me and tried to smile so I continued. "The Canadian Governor General John Buchan said that just before the last war."

"I know, but I hope—"

"Yes, I do too, Tommy. That's why I'm here. We will do our best to hold back the darkness."

"For a big lug you sound a lot like Andy Hardy," he said.

"Then we should be getting costumes for a musical number at the end, right?" This got an all-out laugh from him.

"Okay, you got me," he said. "Let's go and get some food—the coffee at the station is rotting my stomach."

The two of us went out to a diner a block away where we both got milkshakes and hamburgers and for a half-hour, he was able to forget the burden on his shoulders. We talked about his family and his favorite movie stars. I sensed it was the decompression he needed and let the conversation wander to nothing of any consequence.

When we walked back toward the station house, he looked a new man.

"Thank you, Adam," he said. "I appreciate this."

"No thanks necessary," I said, truly glad to see him revived. "I'll keep digging to see if there's any other connection with those occult symbols, any specific direction to go in. And I'm heading to some of the pawnshops on the list from here."

"Great," he said. "Talk to you later."

I watched him walk up the steps and found myself proud that he called me friend. I knew he was a deeply religious man, that my existence was not something he might be able to comprehend yet somehow after Mrs. Kalderash's and Vandoma's acceptance of who and what I was I felt he might not reject me for it.

There was still time to reach a couple of the pawnshops in the Thirties before closing so I walked briskly uptown and over to Sixth Avenue. It was late afternoon with the temperature moderate for February, so the sidewalks were full of busy New Yorkers all going somewhere in a hurry and too busy to notice me. It was how I preferred the streets, where I could feel anonymous.

I visited three of the larger pawnshops on the main avenue, doing my best to be obsequious and act the part of an underworld buyer looking for "something special" with each store owner.

The first store yielded no results, the shopkeeper adhering to good business and the law. The second owner was persuaded to show me a few items that most likely were stolen and not on the "hot sheet" yet— a list of stolen objects that the police circulated to the pawn stores—but

I told him I was not buying that day. The third store practically invited me to buy stolen goods at bargain rates, though no occult objects.

Nico's list will give a lot of business to the police.

The last pawnshop was just off Thirty-Fourth Street on Ninth Avenue, a narrow place, though deep. It was lined with glass display cases showing the talismans of the desperate—watches, gold pens, rings, necklaces, cameos, and one elaborately carved chess set that looked to be of ivory and ebony.

The proprietor was a bald fellow in his dotage whose grey suit looked to be as much an antique as the stuff in the cases. When I entered, he looked up at me and attempted a smile.

"Good afternoon, sir," he said. "How can I help you?"

I did my best to seem friendly. "Hi, I was wondering if you any necklaces for sale."

"Why yes, sir," he said walking back toward me in hopes of making a sale. He stopped at one case of jewelry and pointed. "Some lovely pieces right in here."

"Indeed," I said. "But I was looking for something a little more special." I put emphasis on "special," so much so that he tilted his head.

"I don't take your meaning, sir," he said. I could see the canny thinking, possibly suspecting that I was some agent of the police—which, of course, I was. "All my stock is right here, and it is all very special."

"Ah, I think not quite all," I said, lowering my voice to a confidential tone. "I was led to understand that certain objects—like the particular necklace I am looking for—were only for *special* customers." I let him see a large denomination bill I pulled from a pocket briefly.

He acted obtuse for a few more minutes but I have to assume my better-tailored-than-a-policeman-could-afford suit and my rough features convinced him I was not with the forces of the law. It probably helped that I slipped him a twenty-dollar bill and said, "To help you think a little better."

"Well," he finally said, "I might have one or two special things that I had not put out yet."

Not Born of Woman

He led me to the back of the store where he triggered a hidden panel to a small safe. He was careful to hide the combination. When he turned back, he had a sly smile on his face.

"This what you're looking for?" he asked. He tilted his head to a drawer he'd pulled out where two necklaces and some rings rested.

Neither necklace was the *Koshti Bok*.

"They look good," I said. "But not exactly what I seek; I would like to see some of the things of the kind that the Bund put out the list for."

His eyes went wide, and his hand tightened on the handle of the safe. "How did—?"

"I deal in the same sort of things," I said trying to sound as casual as possible. "And I pay considerably more than those blond fellows can afford."

I'd struck a chord in the pawn dealer; his greed compelled him to push aside any caution that I was a policeman. "Well, I might have one more thing."

He opened a second drawer. "I had promised anything I found like this to those Nazi fellows, but—" He held up a small jade carved figurine slightly smaller than his hand. It was exquisite work, a stylized representation of a jaguar I took to be Aztec or perhaps Mayan.

The remarkable thing was that the figurine shone with light, a soft golden glow that emanated from and surrounded the entire object.

I blinked.

Is that normal?

I had never seen this phenomenon before. It was similar to the phantom forms I sometimes saw surrounding religious figures like Father Burton in that, despite the luminosity, there were no shadows cast from the light.

"It looks beautiful and certainly seems unusual," I said, not wanting to bring up the question of the glow.

"South American," he said with pride. "They say that some witch doctor or such used to wear it in a necklace when he did his conjurations before the heathen masses."

He held it up with a showman's touch to give me a view of all sides. Holding it close to his face made it clear to me that it was indeed some sort of occult aura. There was no reflection of the glow in his glasses and no shadows cast on his face, even though the intensity of the hue would have been bright enough to create such shadows. This made me sure it was an actual occult glow.

This was a new thing to me, this ability to see such occult energy. I assumed it must be related to my visions of the dead, but I had never been in the presence of such objects before and it took me a little aback, though I managed to say, "How much?" to continue the masquerade that I was a criminal buyer.

"Well," he said, pulling it back and suddenly getting cagey as he saw my expression and mistook it for a sale in the making. "I had promised it to those other customers for … well, a tidy sum, but I suppose I could be persuaded and well, what they don't know …"

I kept my focus on the pendant and worked to portray a choosy shopper and so did not react immediately at the bell tinkle of the street door opening. I was only aware that someone had entered when I heard a vaguely familiar voice speak.

"Lock the door, Gunther," the voice said. "We are in luck."

I turned to see three blond men in heavy overcoats, one of whom was locking the door and pulling down the shade. I knew the one who had spoken; he had been in the room with Hans at the Bund headquarters.

"We came for a trinket," the leader said, "but we will also get some excellent revenge!"

CHAPTER TWENTY-FOUR

The storekeeper backed away from me, wringing his hands as he turned toward the three at the other end of the shop.

"What do you mean, Carl?" the keeper asked with fear in his voice. "Why are you here?"

"We came to see if you had acquired anything for us," the leader, Carl, said. He was slightly shorter than his two compatriots though fully as broad shouldered. He smiled like a hungry cat. "And it seems you have brought us a greater treasure than any talisman or cross."

"Yes, you have brought us fresh meat," Gunther, who had locked the door, added. All three men chuckled.

"Gentlemen," the shopkeeper protested. "Please no violence in my store."

The three men ignored the pawnbroker's plea and moved down the narrow store in a wedge formation, as it would not allow them to move more than two abreast. Carl was in the forefront. "If you don't like to watch what's about to happen," the leader said to the shopkeeper, "you can leave out the back."

The store owner blanched with the thought of the inevitable destruction of his business.

"I told you all that you were to stop your ways," I said quietly. "I should think my demonstration with Hans Schmidt would have some impression on you."

"You're going to pay for the other night, *Riesen*," Carl said to me.

"If you leave now, I won't pursue you," I said. "But if you stay, I will be forced to chastise you."

The three all laughed at my statement but before they had enjoyed the jest fully, I lunged forward grabbing Carl's face in my right hand. I yanked him hard, so he flew past me to hit the floor while at the same time I lashed out with my left open hand to slap another of the Nazis across the face. Hard.

The third man grabbed inside his coat and with certainty, it was for a gun.

It didn't matter. I brought my right fist down in a clubbing blow to his right shoulder that partially spun him around and drove him to his knees. I followed that with another open-handed strike that stretched him out unconscious on the floor of the store.

I spun then to look to Carl who was now on his feet. He had pulled a gun but instead of pointing it at me had pressed it to the back of the terrified storekeeper.

"Back away from me, *Riesen*," Carl snapped. His eyes were wide and fearfully darting left and right.

"Let him go, Nazi," I said. There was no mercy in my tone.

"You do not order the master race, swine," he said.

"You cannot even master your fear," I said. "You are a master of nothing but hate and vileness. A coward who covers his weakness with bluster." I moved slowly toward him, and I'm sure my expression was not a pleasant one.

"Back!" Carl yelled and pushed the shopkeeper to the ground to point the gun at me. "Back!" He yelled as he pulled the trigger twice to fire at me.

Whether from fear or incompetence his aim was terrible. One bullet whizzed past my left cheek and the second hit me in the left side but low near my hip.

I sprang forward at him then and wrapped my larger hand around his smaller one holding the gun and yanked hard. There was a snap and a yell from him, his eyes now wide with pain and a deeper terror as he was close to me.

"I warned you," I said with no warmth in my voice. "Now you've made me angry."

Not Born of Woman

Suddenly there was blinding pain and I felt my legs go weak. I dropped to my knees and was vaguely aware of the storekeeper standing beside me with a heavy urn in his hands.

"Get out of my store," the pawnbroker yelled to the Bundists. "You'll bring the police down on me."

Carl who was crying now, blubbering incoherently, paused to kick me in the side then grabbed his fallen pistol—a Mauser, I noted through my pain—with his left hand. He called to the other two Bundists and then the three of them raced out of the store.

I forced myself to my feet and turned to the shopkeeper who still held the bronze urn. "You get away from me," he said. "You and those damn Nazis—stay away from me."

I was unsteady on my feet and leaned on the counter. I now realized that my side was bleeding, and the paint of it was white hot.

"You would do yourself a service to stop dealing with criminals," I said. "This stolen pendant needs to be the last of its kind." I reached past him and took the jaguar pendant. "Swear you'll stop now, and I will not talk to the police."

He stared at me with a growing horror that I was looming over him and seemed suddenly aware that, though wounded, I was still capable of ending him.

"I ... I ... I swear." He crossed himself and backed away from me. His eyes looked down to the pendant and back to my eyes and I saw there was sincerity in his denial, though how long prudence would hold out over greed was anyone's guess.

I turned away from him and walked out of the store into the darkness of the early evening crowd feeling like I had failed again.

I took a taxi to my office feeling odd from the whole experience. Mort's Drugstore was still open, but I chose to head directly upstairs to assess my wound.

At my office door, I stopped long enough to check that my security hair was there; it was not.

This stopped me.

I paused and waited, listening at the door. I detected no sound, so I chanced to unlock the door, and stepped in, reaching to turn on the light as I did.

Vandoma's office was empty, so I moved swiftly to the doorway to the inner room. There too I snapped on the light and lunged around the door.

The inner office was empty as well.

Why would someone break in here? What did they take? Or—what did they leave?

I spent several minutes walking the perimeter of the room looking for anything out of place that had been moved or added to the room. All the books were where I remembered, the chairs and the rest seemed to be as they had been.

I'll have to look again later, this pain in my side is too much to ignore. I have to deal with this.

I removed my coat, vest, and jacket, dropping them all by the door, and fell heavily into my desk chair. I opened my shirt and looked to my side.

My flesh, pale at all times, seemed more so with a neat hole just above my hip. When I felt behind, there was no exit wound; instead, I felt a sore spot with what seemed an odd bump.

So, it had not been a "through and through" as I had heard Tommy call wounds where a bullet passed cleanly through flesh.

I removed my shirt and went into the washroom where I had a small first aid kit. I procured a small knife and forceps. When I twisted to look in the mirror at my back I could see the odd protrusion, like a pebble beneath my skin. The bullet had passed through my lateral oblique muscle but had not damaged anything internally, as far as I could discern, and through happenstance had lost so much velocity that it could not exit my skin.

I poured some alcohol on the knife, gritted my teeth and made an incision next to the nodule, and then, using the forceps, reached beneath the skin to pull out the bullet.

Not Born of Woman

I had to stifle a groan of pain but continued, letting my mind concentrate on a poem by Gibran. "Your pain is the breaking of the shell that encloses your understanding." I hoped I would find understanding for the foolish encounter with the Bundists.

Still, the pain was bearable. My only real concern was for cloth fibers in the wound that could fester. I cleaned the hole as thoroughly as possible and applied some sulfur powder antiseptic to it.

I had enough bandages in the cabinet to secure the wound and wrap myself, at least until Dottie could check my handiwork. I knew from my own constitution—via my creator's hands—that the injury would heal in a reasonable time if it did not become infected. I would see Dottie in a day or two and keep an eye on it until then.

I sat back gingerly in my desk chair, feeling more tired than I could remember, and set the bullet down on the desk to stare at it. So remarkable that a little piece of lead could take so many lives. I was glad I had missed the carnage of what they called the Great War while I was still in isolation and tried to imagine how many lives had been lost because of those dollops of lead.

My head was spinning with all the threads that had spun off my agreement to find the Kalderash *Koshti Bok*. There was a killer or killers apparently looking to acquire occult powers from deaths and at the same time, the Nazis were also in the market for objects of power. I removed the jade jaguar from my pants pocket and set it on my desk next to the bullet and the book that Digger had gifted me, the *Amuletae boni et mali*.

Such an unholy trinity; how do you all connect?

With no real idea what to do next and my side throbbing, I opened the book to look through it in the hope that I might find something like the jaguar in it. In a short time, I was rewarded.

"There you are!" I said out loud about halfway through the book.

There was an engraving of the jade object as part of an elaborate necklace that had been recorded by a Jesuit missionary in the 1600s in Mexico. According to the priest who drew it—after confiscating it for the Vatican—it was said to be used to communicate with Aztec Gods. The Vatican had declared it evil and that it should be destroyed.

It seemed likely that instead it was broken apart and it was possible that only this single jaguar was all that had survived.

I had taken off my gloves to minister to myself so when I picked up the jaguar and held the glowing thing, I felt a strange warmth from it. Not exactly heat but a tingling feeling that communicated to me that there was indeed power in this object.

So, these occult things are real.

And why not? Most would agree that I could not exist in this modern world of science and logic, yet I did. There was no longer a reason to doubt such power and now it made the Nazi's quest for such objects all the more frightening for the havoc they could wreak with such power at their command.

I set the jaguar down on the desk and ran a hand over the open *Amuletae boni et mali*.

What can you tell me? Is this magic the reason I exist?

As I turned the pages looking at the objects said to have so much power, I reached the picture of the *Koshti Bok* of the Kalderash family. Once more I looked at the Hebrew writing in the margins that I'd been having trouble reading. I ran my hand over the page, and I noticed something odd.

There were impressions on the page—shallow indentations on the paper. I ran my fingers along them, and it became clear that someone had traced the outlines of the figures of the Hebrew glyphs on the page. The exact outline of the Hebrew words, in fact.

So, this is why someone broke in here. I had not been imagining it when I thought the book had been moved. Someone had been looking through the book and had particularly paused on this page and copied the material. It made reading the Hebrew text even more important.

Dare I ask Mort to help me translate this? I did not want to involve him further in my troubles, but if this passage about the *Koshti Bok* was important enough for someone to break into my office I had to know why.

How did they even know I had this book? Could someone have traced it to Digger and then to me?

My side was throbbing, but I put it out of my mind. I took a sheet of paper and decided to split the difference between revealing the contents to Mort and waiting until I was educated enough to read it myself. Instead, I copied the first few lines of the handwritten notes in the margin.

I set the book back on the desk and placed the *Amuletae boni et mali* very precisely, taking careful note of where the edges aligned and putting a hair in a specific page that might not be noticed by any trespassers.

I tucked in my shirt and donned a clean jacket and vest, then reset my "security" hair in the door before heading downstairs. I had a feeling that things were coming to a head.

CHAPTER TWENTY-FIVE

Mort was about to close up the drug store when I entered.

"Hello, Adam," he called from where he was arranging boxes on a shelf in the pharmacy area behind his counter. "Did you have a full day?"

I had to laugh. "You might say that, Mort." My side hurt enough that I sat on a stool at the soda counter.

Jake was closing down the counter, actually on his knees behind it, stacking glasses and putting cardboard delivery containers away. He looked up to see me.

"Hi, Mister P," he said. "Can I get you something?"

"No, I'm fine, Jake. I just came in to see if there were any messages."

"Yup, sure," the teenager popped up. "I took one about an hour ago." He searched around in the pocket of his apron until he pulled out a scrap of paper that he held out to me.

His scrawl was childish, but I recognized the number; it was Vandoma's. I headed to the phone booth right away.

"Hello, this is the home of the Kalderash family."

"Hello, Vandoma?"

"Mister Paradise," she said, her voice sounding relieved. "It is good to hear your voice."

"Is everything all right?"

"Yes," she said, "My brother is home, and he has told me and my mother of the Manzetti man and how you saved him. My gratitude is—"

"Please, Vandoma," I said, "there is nothing to thank me for."

"Yes, Mister Paradise, there is." Her voice was full of emotion. "My brother has renounced his ways and my mother feels he has come home to the tribe as he should be. This is much."

I was daunted for a moment to reply but finally managed, "I'm glad I could help."

"Is there much progress?" she asked as if to deflect from the emotion in the conversation.

"Not at the moment," I said. I had decided not to tell her about my run-in with the Bundists at the pawnshop. "But I am about to go to Tommy at the police to see what they're doing."

She then said, hesitantly, "My mother has seen a thing."

"A thing?"

"She saw the *Koshti Bok* in your hands," she said, "but she saw that there was blood on it. This is a frightening thing, for she does not know whose blood it was. I worry that it was yours."

I absorbed this for a moment before I answered. "Don't worry about that. That blood may well be because of the criminal who stole it in the first place."

I felt a twinge of guilt for not telling her of my new wound and also a little chill that her mother had possibly seen that event since I was in pursuit of the necklace. I had little doubt of her mother's power now.

"Please be careful, Mister Paradise," she said. "Promise you will?"

"I promise I will, and I'll call you if there's any news."

She hung up and I stayed, pressed into the phone booth for a moment while staring at the receiver.

I will do my best not to fail you, Vandoma.

When I came out of the phone booth, Mort had finished behind the drug counter and came to join me as I sat on a stool at the soda counter.

"How are you, my friend?" he asked.

"Just a little worse for wear, Mort, and I know I said there was no time for our lesson, but I was hoping you might be able to translate these symbols for me." I pushed the sheet of paper I'd traced the Hebrew script onto across the counter.

"Geeze," Jake asked, "what's that?" He set aside his apron and the cap he wore when working and peered in to look at my drawings.

"Hmm," Mort said, leaning in to study them. "You were right, it is Hebrew script, Adam, but it is early Hebrew, what some call the Canaanite Hebrew alphabet."

"Can you decipher it?"

He stroked his chin and stared at the sketches with deep concentration. "It is a development from the Aramaic alphabet that evolved during the Persian, Hellenistic, and Roman periods. This is very early script though with much of the Paleo-Hebrew alphabet. It is very old."

"But can you read it?" I asked. "I think it has a bearing on the case I'm working on; it was why I wanted to begin my lessons, but things have become … uh … urgent."

"This would take more than a few lessons, my friend." He looked up at me and gave a wry smile. "Early Hebrew exists in a variety of local variants and shows development over time. I have studied Early Hebrew writing, the Gezer Calendar which dates from the tenth-century BCE. Yet this is very unique."

"How so?"

"It seems to be a phrase referring to death and power," he said. "But in odd combination—almost a Kabalistic arraignment."

"Kabalistic?" Jake asked.

"The Jewish Kabbalah is a set of esoteric teachings that explain the relationship between the unchanging, eternal God—*Ein Sof*, 'The Infinite'—and the mortal, finite universe that is his creation."

"Golly," Jake said, "Pretty strange stuff."

"It's a form of occult knowledge, is it not?" I asked.

"Yes," Mort answered. "It dates from the twelfth century, but this script is older—so that is a puzzle."

"So, an ancient knowledge that predates even the Kabbalah?"

"It would seem so," Mort said. "It is a theory of the ten creative forces that intervene between the infinite and finite and how to manipulate them. Life and death are opposites, but these forces can unite them, even subvert them." He looked up at me with a serious expression. "This is only a part of the phrase, of course, but I think I can read it better if I consult some books."

Not Born of Woman

"I would appreciate it," I said. "I have to go out again, but I'll be coming back here later. Perhaps you can look at it tonight to tell me what you found tomorrow?"

"Certainly," he said. "I have books at home I can consult."

"Thank you." I rose and waved to both of them. "Good night."

"Night, Mister P."

"Good night, Adam," Mort said. "And don't worry, there is no puzzle that cannot be solved."

I wish I had your faith, my friend.

"This little thing is stolen?" Tommy asked me as he held the jade jaguar.

"I would bet on it," I said. We were in his office, his desk piled with coffee cups and paperwork. I told him of my run-in with the Bundists, though not yet that I had been shot. "The pawnshop dealer was eager to unload it on me and the Nazis would have bought it, I'm sure."

"Might have been stolen from out of town or a private collector who has not reported it."

"Especially if that collector also got it illegally."

"Exactly," Tommy said. "I'll get it over to the robbery detail and they can make some calls."

"Good. I have something else for you to look at," I pulled the bullet from my jacket pocket and held it up. "It's from a Mauser."

He looked shocked and took it from me to examine it. "Where did you—?"

"Same Nazis," I said.

"It's not deformed," he said, his eyes narrowing. "But it's been fired—what was it fired into?" When I didn't answer he asked, "Or who was it fired into?"

"It was only a slight wound," I said. "Really."

He did not look happy. "You're a jerk," he said. Then he was all business. "Definitely a Mauser?"

"Yes, and I can identify the man who fired it if that becomes necessary.'

"Necessary? He shot you."

"Yes, but what profit to prosecute him for that? It will only matter if that gun is the one that shot Dorfman, Father Burton, and the others."

"Well, they were all shot with the same gun as Dorfman," he said. "That much is certain; ballistics confirmed it."

"Then this bullet could close the case if …."

He went to the door and called out, "Callahan?"

A young officer came running at the call. "Yes, sir?"

"Take this personally over to ballistics and have them run a test on it to see if it matches those bullets from the priest killing."

The officer's eyes went wide. "Yes sir," he said and hurried off.

"And keep the chain of evidence, okay?" Tommy called.

"How long do you think it will take?" I asked when he rejoined me at his desk.

"They'll jump on this," he said. "They are keeping the lab open because of the girls and now Father Burton. Maybe half an hour. It would be a huge break if this is the gun. Now tell me the details."

I was forced then to divulge all that occurred at the pawnshop. When I was done, he shook his head.

"You're nuts, Adam. I don't care how scary you can look, going up against three of those Nazi crazies is—well, crazy."

I had to laugh. "It did seem like the thing to do at the time, and after all, I got a nice souvenir out of it for you."

He laughed. "Crazy!"

Just then the phone on his desk rang.

"Shane," he said. "Yes—yes? He's here. Okay." He looked up at me. "It's for you!"

"No one knew I was here," I said. I put the phone to my ear. "This is Adam Paradise."

"It's him, boss," a strange voice said and then the receiver at the other end of the phone was handed off.

"Mister Paradise." It was Guido.

"Mister Manzetti," I said. "To what do I owe this surprising call?"

Not Born of Woman

"I do not like it when my employees, present or past act without my knowledge or permission. Such an occurrence has happened."

"I understand," I said. "No prejudice for their actions."

"It has come to my attention that Mickey Castliano, who used to work for me and who you know, has communicated with those *vaffanculo* Nazis and told them about the Gypsy and where he lives."

"I thank you very much for this information, sir."

"Mister Castliano will not inform on anyone again, by the way," he said, almost casually. "I thought you'd like to act on the information about the Gyspy."

"Indeed, I do. As always, sir, you are a professional and a gentleman. And I am in your debt."

"Yes, you are." He said then hung up.

A chill went down my spine.

"Can I get an outside line on this?" I asked Tommy. He could see from my expression I was concerned.

"Just dial nine," he said.

I did and then called the Kalderash number. There was a busy signal. I told Tommy who had called and where I was trying to call.

"I need to get through," I said to him. "Can I get you to break through on this?"

"Hang up and give me the number, Adam." He took the phone from me and put through a call to an operator, got a supervisor on the call, and invoked his credentials.

After what seemed an eternal wait the operator came on and he nodded and said, "Thanks."

Then he looked at me. "The phone is off the hook, Adam."

"I have to get there."

"We'll take an unmarked radio car," he said as he grabbed his coat and hat. "It has a siren."

CHAPTER TWENTY-SIX

The ride to the Kalderash home in Long Island City in Queens seemed interminable to me. We took the Fifty-Ninth Street Bridge with Tommy using the siren most of the way to part the February traffic. In the car, we traveled in silence with my friend concentrating on driving and myself lost in dark thoughts.

Have I brought the vengeance of the Nazis down on the Kalderash family? Regardless that Nico had begun this with his careless gambling, I fear that my punitive assault on the Bundists has predicated some form of attack on the family.

In all my time back among mankind, I had never felt so much fear for those around me. In my few years in New York, I had begun to feel a part of a community and now that is all threatened. I was chilled to the bone to think that the Roma woman who had come to me for help could be hurt by my own childish hubris in resorting to violence.

Tommy cut the siren when we came off the bridge and even cut his headlights as we rolled to a stop down the block from the Kalderash's A-frame home.

"Let me go first, Adam," Tommy said in a near whisper when we approached the building. He drew his pistol.

"We don't know for sure what to expect," I said, trying to convince myself as much as him and terrified for what we might find. "It might be nothing."

"Or it might be something, so follow my lead," he said. "I'm the professional at this, okay?"

Not Born of Woman

I deferred to him, so we moved up to either side of the front door. He looked down at the doorknob indicating I should proceed. I nodded, reaching out to touch it. It turned easily and the door opened.

I pulled it wide, and Tommy darted in, moving low with his gun held out at the ready.

I followed immediately into the foyer and knew at once that things were very wrong from the odd lighting coming from the interior.

The inner door to the hall was broken and off the hinges. Tommy looked back at me with concern, and I nodded for him to proceed.

The hallway was dark, lit only by flickering firelight coming from the sitting room. A side table in the hall was overturned and chairs in the living room were knocked over, everything in disarray. I moved ahead of Tommy into the kitchen while he went into the sitting room.

In the kitchen, I did a quick survey to find that it was empty with everything in order and the back door was securely locked from within.

"Adam!" Tommy called from the sitting room with such urgency in his voice that I raced back. Inside the room I found my friend kneeling behind one of the overturned chairs next to a still form that, as I got closer, I could see was Mother Kalderash.

The old Roma was unmoving on her left side facing the fire, looking so small and frail with the shadows of the flames dancing over her in shifting patterns. I could see there was an ugly purple bruise that ran the entire length of the exposed side of her face.

I felt an abrupt pain in my stomach and a swelling of anger with an icicle of fear in my heart. "Beasts!"

Tommy seemed afraid to touch her. He looked up at me and I saw his eyes glance back toward the stairs.

"I'll check upstairs," he whispered. His expression was grim.

"I'll stay with her," I replied and knelt by the old woman as he went up to search the second floor.

I removed my right-hand glove and reached out with fear to touch the old woman's throat. It was still warm, and I felt the throb of blood, weakly, pulsing beneath the skin. As I set my coat over her, she moaned softly.

"Nico," she whispered, "Vandoma …."

"Easy, Mother Kalderash," I said. "We're looking for them."

"The *gadjo* of the broken cross took them," she said in Romani. She turned her head to glance up at me, her eyes looking not just at me but beyond as well. "They said this was to punish you *Martja* but this was to their shame, their *ladz*. They are dogs, not men. They said they take them to the dragonslayer."

"No one here," Tommy said as he returned, stopping when he saw she was moving. "They tore out the phone; I'll have to go out to the car to radio for an ambulance. I'll put out a dragnet for them—see what information you can get from her."

"The Nazis," I said. "It was the Nazis."

When he was gone, she reached up a hand and gripped my bare hand with surprising strength. "This is just *gadzikani baxt*, bad luck, *pajivalo Martja*, do not fear for me." She gave a grimace that might have been an attempt at a smile.

"Quiet, Mother," I whispered. "Save your strength; help will come."

"No, *Murtja*," she said. "I am *chovuhanis*, a healer. I know that my time here is done."

"No, Mother—"

"I am also *drukker*—I see the future. You must listen; the *Koshti Bok*—it is a danger to my children. The luck of my family is now the danger. Vandoma and Nico, you must save them. You must stop the living earth that comes for them." Her eyes bored into me with an internal light and her voice gained strength. "You will find that truth is your salvation. You are *familija* now, you must find them."

"*Solax*," I whispered to her compliment of including me in her extended family. "I take an oath."

She grimaced in pain then her features relaxed. As I watched, the light slowly faded out of her eyes. She gave a heave letting out her last breath, a long low hissing sound as life escaped her.

I saw close-up the moment when her spirit left her body. It took the form of a luminosity that floated up from her. I had seen it before but now, for the first time ever I saw a recognizable figure that ascended. It was like an image of the dead woman, formed as if in translucent smoke. It drifted up from her, not the black and crimson of others that had died from violence. This time the image that rose was a golden and

Not Born of Woman

amber phantom where the features were clearly that of expired Mother Kalderash.

As I watched, the ghostly form—for that is clearly what it was—turned toward me and appeared to smile. Then like real smoke, it dissipated to the amorphous glow I was familiar with and that I now knew with certainty was the essence of the dead. I felt a cold sensation wash over me, but I knew it was not borne of the material world.

"I called for an ambulance," Tommy said as he raced back in.

"No need to hurry," I said rising. "The lady has departed."

He stood for a second and crossed himself, his expression darkening. "Did—did she say anything?"

"She just said men of the broken cross—Nazis—did this. And they did it to punish me."

"Easy, Adam, don't put this on yourself."

"How can I not? If I had not angered them—"

"Don't go down that road, Adam. Don't! Those kinds of thugs do what they do with no real need for justification." He came over and crossed himself again over the body of the old woman and we stood for a moment in silence.

"Did she have any idea where the son and your lady have gone?"

"She said only that they were taken," I said. I tried to parse her words. "And something else ... is there a Lithuanian community around here?"

"Not that I know of," he said.

"Anywhere associated with St.George? That saint is a patron of Lithuania."

"What?"

"Of Saint George and the dragon. She said they were taken to the Dragonslayer."

He thought a moment. "There is a St. George section on Staten Island."

"That could be it," I said, but it didn't feel right to me. I thought a bit more. "Wait—maybe the wrong mythology."

"What do you mean?" he asked.

"Well, the Nazis are all about their supposed Teutonic heritage, the imagined glorious past of their own created mythology. And they are into Richard Wagner."

"Who?"

"An opera composer."

"That leaves me out," he said.

Despite it all, I gave a slight smile and continued, "Wagner wrote *Di Walkure, Der Ring des Nibelungen* and *Gotterdammerung*." He looked at me uncomprehendingly. "The Ring Cycle. All about a mythical hero who slays a dragon and gets occult powers."

"Like Saint George?"

"Sort of. And his name was Siegfried." I saw his expression change.

"Like Camp Siegfried!" he said.

"Yes," I exclaimed, "that has to be it!"

The German American Bund maintained two summer camp compounds—one in New Jersey called Camp Nordland and one on Long Island called Camp Siegfried.

"That's out in Yaphank," he said with excitement. "Part of Brookhaven, I think."

"How long is it to drive from here?"

"Oh, at night? Maybe two hours or so. I have no idea how bad the roads are."

"I have to go there," I said. "If there is a chance they're there—"

"Yeah, I get it," he said. "Let me put out another call then—"

"No," I said. "I need to go alone; besides you need to stay here for the paperwork, right?"

He looked me in the eye and saw I would brook no argument. "Okay—let me make that call then and take this—" He offered me his pistol.

"No, thank you," I said. "I don't like guns and am more likely to hurt myself than any Nazis."

We went out to the car where he put in another call to his dispatcher and then showed me how to operate the radio. He also gave me his call sign.

"If you get in trouble, use my name," he said. "I've made sure that if any local cops stop you, I've cleared that you have the car."

Not Born of Woman

I adjusted the seat, sliding it back so my legs were not cramped while driving.

"I'll be on my way to you as soon as I get some units here to cover this scene," Tommy said. "Keep the radio turned on, though I don't know what range it will have. I'll call you when I'm on the way. Oh, and there's a road map of the state in the glove compartment, that may help."

"Thank you, Tommy."

"Don't thank me and then go get yourself killed, Adam. I still haven't beaten you enough at chess."

I nodded and then put the car in gear to head out to what I suspected would be my own *Gotterdammerung*. It didn't matter, as long as I was in time to save Vandoma and her brother.

CHAPTER TWENTY-SEVEN

The borough of Queens gave way to the suburban and then the semi-rural as I drove East on Long Island toward the town of Yaphank. Since 1936, the Bund had run summer camps across the nation that were similar to Hitler Youth Camps back in Germany. Camp Siegfried even had its own dedicated train on the Long Island Railroad called the "Siegfried Special." They had a pool, archery competitions, hikes through the woods, a Youth Camp on the other side of Upper Lake and ran all sorts of family-oriented activities.

They were even building a Germanic community around the camp. A number of people had become alarmed—especially after the big rally at Madison Square Garden—by the influence and power of the American Bund and how much allegiance they owed to the Fatherland and Hitler.

According to a court case brought the year before by New York's Secretary of State against the German American Settlement League, they were in violation of the Civil Rights Law of 1923, which had been created to control the Ku Klux Klan. They said that to become a member of the Bund one had to swear allegiance to Hitler and to the leaders of the German American Bund. During the trial, a witness was asked to demonstrate how those at the camp saluted the American flag and he responded by giving the Nazi salute. When asked if this was "the American salute," the witness responded, "It will be."

This was the mentality I was up against; these were the people who had kidnapped the Kalderash siblings.

Not Born of Woman

As I drove out, I listened to the police radio, but it sputtered out not long after and there was only silence and darkness. And my thoughts.

The Nazis wanted to punish me for crossing them but why not just kill Vandoma and Nico at their home? If it was just to hurt me, that would have sufficed, would it not? Then why take them?

I thought back to the rehearsal for the ceremony that Hans and his cronies had just finished when I reached the roof of their headquarters.

That was where they had mentioned Siegfried.

The full moon was up which made driving the rural roads a little easier, but I still had to stop several times to read road signs and consult the map from the glove compartment. It was not detailed enough to give me the location of the camp, however. I was able to locate a conveniently open gas station after a time and they had a more accurate local map that helped me stay on the right path.

The eeriness of the moonlight on the flat, winter landscape made me think of the long winter nights and days in the arctic and all the time alone, thinking that I would ever be alone, always, and into the greater dark that was beyond. Then I was not aware of the true nature of the vague amorphous phantoms I observed around me and that I found hovering around the icebound ship I had taken refuge in. I didn't know—as I now knew with irrefutable proof after Mother Kalderash's death—that there was a continuance after this consciousness.

And then, when I lay for weeks recovering from my fight with the polar bear, some of the time delirious and with no real hope of anything more, I cared little to continue—yet life persisted despite my lack of caring whether I did or not.

Even when I longed to end my loneliness, the will to live continued and I survived.

Now I knew that there was something more, that even if my eyes closed for the last time in this world there might be another and so what I had come to hold precious, my very existence, was not a finite thing. I had always been aware that I had no idea how long my "natural-unnatural" life would continue—the two centuries it already had without aging, or a hundred. Would I still walk the dying earth when mankind's candle had been extinguished and if so—why?

Now I drove to confront the Nazis in their lair, with no illusion that this time I could leave it without greater violence than I had encountered before. I was not going to teach them a lesson or reason with them. There was no reasoning with beasts and these Bundists had surrendered their reason to the vilest of instincts at the bestial level. It was highly likely I was facing death.

Surprisingly, I felt no apprehension; Mother Kaldersah's death had removed any fear of losing this consciousness, this iteration of who I was. In fact, the opposite, as I now felt there was a reason I was there in that car, on that drive, attempting to give surcease to Vandoma and Nico.

Once again, I thought of Nietzche's words, "He who has a why to live can bear almost any how." I now had a why. Vandoma had given me that when she walked into my office. I could no longer believe that all the things that led her to me, that my friendship with Tommy Shane or my office being where it was, even my being in New York were all coincidences.

If ever I doubted the hands of some creator larger than Victor Frankenstein's, I had no such doubts now. If I had no purpose in existence greater than being able to help Vandoma, then so be it. The French Jesuit said, "The world is round so that friendship may encircle it." And she was my friend. No price was too high to pay for her safety.

As I approached the area of the camp, the effects of the hurricane from the year before—now called the Long Island Express—became visible. The hurricane swept up the coast to northern latitudes from the Caribbean and ultimately killed almost seven hundred people, just missing New York City and slicing through the center of Long Island, devastating the Eastern end and destroying much property.

The rapid forward motion of this storm made warnings all but impossible.

Not Born of Woman

The eye of the hurricane came ashore at Bayport not far east of the Camp and the foliage and terrain still reflected that. I was forced to move slowly with some roads still in terrible shape and make a detour before I was close enough to the camp to stop.

I parked my car a quarter mile from the camp, pulling off the gravel road to conceal the sedan. I positioned it in a copse of trees pointing outward in anticipation of a quick getaway. There was no radio signal at all, it had faded out long before I reached my destination.

I had left my trench coat over the body of Mother Kalderash, so I had only my suit jacket against the February weather. The wind itself did not bother me. I was more concerned that my white shirt was a bit bright. The ground was still very moist from the rain the day before, so I found some mud and smeared it on the shirtfront and for good measure on my face to disguise my whiteness, in the same way that soldiers did when going into combat. I grinned when I thought of what a ragged image I would present when I finally found Vandoma.

I walked along the shoulder of the gravel road, in the grass to keep the sound of my passage down, and in doing so stumbled on a canvas-covered truck that was also pulled off the road into the underbrush as if in an attempt to hide it.

Out of curiosity, I gave it a cursory examination. I noted that the tire tracks dug deeply into the ground indicating it was carrying heavy cargo, yet when I peered in the back it was empty. I saw some drag marks or deep impressions leaving the truck, so it appeared that the cargo had been removed, though there were no wheel marks.

Reaching into the back of the truck I found some smears of clay but nothing else to indicate what the vehicle had been carrying.

There was nothing in the cab to indicate whose truck it was, so I moved on. Considering that there could be any number of reasons the Bundists had parked a truck outside their compound, I had no reason to dally.

Camp Siegfried was in a very rural area of Suffolk County with low hills around it. The vast tract of land contained a parade ground and parking lots. It was really a little town of log buildings and wooden shacks laid out on streets with names like "Hitler Way," "Goebbels Lane," and "Göring Road." There was a wide gate with a sign proclaiming the name of the camp and its sponsorship by 'The German American Settlement League.'

The moon was near its zenith as I moved along the side of a gravel road that led to the main entrance to the camp compound. There was a long, low barbed wire fence that extended around the camp but seemed more to keep animals out than for any real security. There was, however, a manned guard post at the gate so I moved along the fence line until I was concealed and far enough from them to make no telltale sounds when I jumped over the fence.

The bullet wound in my side only gave a slight twinge when I vaulted the fence, but it did not hamper my movements, so I kept going.

Once inside the compound, I saw a large number of cars parked in the open area beyond the gate. I kept clear of them and made swiftly to the side of one of the log buildings, as the gibbous moon was so bright that the whole of the camp was illuminated almost like day. There was no movement visible along the wide avenue but the smoke drifting up from the chimneys of several of the wooden shacks—built mostly for the summer camp activities—showed there were fires in them.

There seems to be a large gathering of the Nazis tonight.

I cast my mind to what I knew of the occult and its practices. The full moon is the time of the month when some believe that energy peaks and releases its powers to those who call on it. This originated in places like Egypt and Babylonia in cultures that worshipped the moon.

If the Nazis were using stolen occult objects for their powers, it would make sense that they would use them on such a night. And that practice ceremony I had come upon would seem to portend such an affair.

But where would they do it? And where would they keep prisoners?

I was reduced to lurking from cabin to cabin, bending low and running from window to window to see who was inside. I observed half a dozen or so individuals in each shack or cabin, both men and women, all of a Nordic type; most wore military-style uniforms with Swastikas on armbands.

The snatches of conversation I heard were all inconsequential, even trivialities, both in English and German with topics ranging from "who is cute" and "who is a jerk" to political statements about how "we have to kick the fools out of city hall" or "when we take over Washington."

It was not until I reached the fourth building, a slightly larger cabin I came upon from the moon-shadowed side, that I heard what I hoped to.

"Hurry up and get the robes, Fritz," one voice said. "We only have a half-hour until we're to assemble for the ritual."

"But won't the fact that they are *Zigeuners* foul the ritual?" one of those in the cabin said. *Zigeuner* was the German word for a male Roma.

"No," someone answered with a laugh. "There are purebloods who are dedicating themselves as well. The *Zigeuner* and his bitch will fill in for the dog sacrifices the old rituals call for." This was followed by general laughter within.

I was enraged.

It was all I could do to contain my anger and keep myself from bursting into the building to chastise the Nazis, but it would gain me nothing. I needed to know where the siblings were being held and any violence at all to extract information would bring the force of the camp down on me and thwart that aim.

I swallowed my bile and waited, crouching beneath the window in hopes of hearing more that might give me some clue where Vandoma and her brother were.

I was concentrating so much on listening to the inside of the cabin that I had not been vigilant about my surroundings. Now I heard a footstep from the end of the building as someone rounded the far corner coming in my direction!

CHAPTER TWENTY-EIGHT

The person rounding the corner was a young man in a heavy coat who was occupied with lighting a cigarette, so his focus was down on the tip, hand cupped to shield a match flame from the wind.

This gave me a split second to launch myself at him.

By the time he realized there was movement in the shadow of the building I was upon him and with no time to be subtle I clubbed him to the ground. I palmed his face, crushing the cigarette into his cheek, and dragged him beside the building.

The man was terrified, his eyes wide with fear of me and I used this.

"Where are the two prisoners?" I whispered into his ear.

He made to moan and tried to wiggle free. I used my other hand to squeeze his neck.

"Make no sound above a whisper or just point to where they are." My face was right beside his and I am sure I looked more beast than man with my mud-smeared face. "And if you cry out, I will end you."

He tentatively extended his left hand to indicate a direction. "The stone house," he whispered.

I clubbed him unconscious with little finesse and it is possible I did major damage to him, but I had to consider the possibility of him waking up before I could find the Roma. I then tied his hands behind him using his belt and used his tie as a gag. I rolled him flush against the base of the cabin and then headed off in the direction he had indicated.

There was a stone building at the head of a row of cabins which from all indications was some sort of community hall. It was two stories tall and had a large Swastika inlaid in the eave over the wide, double doors.

Unfortunately, I would have to pass across a large parade ground-like space with a flagpole in the center of it to reach the building. It was some sort of ad hoc town square situated across from the perpendicularly set rows of cabins.

I saw no lights in the stone structure but that didn't mean that someone wasn't looking out. I reasoned that a skulking figure would look suspicious, but that a figure walking boldly and relaxed across the space would look like they belonged, perhaps a Bundist out for a night's stroll or coming to participate in the ceremony.

To that end, I straightened up and walked directly across the open space as if I did not have a care in the world.

I walked directly up to the building's front door, but it was locked. I flattened against the side of the structure and walked along the perimeter. I saw no lights through any windows of the ground floor rooms as I walked around half the building. I noticed that all the windows had large, heavy storm shutters outside them, I assume in reaction to last year's hurricane.

Just as I rounded the second corner, I saw a faint glow from a room ahead.

I paused and listened.

Nothing.

I cautiously slid along the wall to the edge of the window and peeked around to look into the room.

Inside was a large space that looked like a lecture hall. A group of chairs all pointed up toward a stage on which a long table was set in such a way to remind me of a church's altar, complete with a white cloth that had a Swastika embroidered down the front of it in red draped over it. Behind the table was a large portrait of Adolph Hitler with American and German flags flanking the portrait.

The light I had detected came from the top of that altar-like table. It was a soft, almost ambient light that pulsed now amber, now golden, now tinted green.

Just like the Jade Jaguar.

I suddenly knew I had to get into that room and get whatever objects of power that the Nazis had accumulated and then get the Kalderash out of the camp.

This is a place of evil.

Many will say that the very concept of evil is a relative thing, as is the concept of good. What is good for one civilization can be the destruction of another. Countries in war must find a way to demonize the enemy—make them the *other*. It was what the Nazis had done to literally everyone who was not them.

As I pried open the window and climbed into the lecture room, I realized I felt a palpable sense of evil in that room. An absolute evil! I felt it as if it was a physical thing.

It was true that by their own rationale, the Nazis had made themselves the *evil* to everyone else. In that space, the temple to their Teutonic cause, they had filled the room with the essence of their hate and insecurity and I felt it.

When I reached the stage, I saw what was glowing; there was a large medieval dagger, a chalice, and a golden spear lain out on the altar as if in ritual readiness. Each had slightly different hues radiating from them—the dagger a distinctly greenish tint, the chalice pure golden, and the spear actually showed a slight hint of red in the amber that pulsed from it.

There was more, however, for from both the spear point and knife, there were vague wisps as if of smoke puffs, rising upward from them and all but invisible to me in the darkened room. When I looked up to follow their course I saw, hovering near the ceiling, the shapes I knew were the remnants of murder victims. Black, crimson, and indigo phantoms told me each of the weapons had taken many lives.

Ritual instruments of death!

I knew all the more that I had to take these things and quickly find the Kalderash siblings, or a terrible fate awaited them.

As I reached for the dagger the auditorium was suddenly ablaze with light.

The doors at the back of the room flung open and armed Nazis burst into the room.

Not Born of Woman

I was caught like a butterfly pinned in the light with Thomson submachine guns pointed at me.

"Do not even try to escape, *Riesen*," Hans' voice boomed from the back of the room. "Or Gunther will kill the *Zigeuerin*."

At that moment one of the Bundists stepped into the room with a pistol at Vandoma's temple. The gleeful expression on his face told me he was not bluffing.

Now Hans entered, careful not to block the machine guns pointed at me. He was in a Nazi uniform with both his arms in casts. His smile was wide.

"Stefan foiled you, *Riesen*," Hans said. "When we found him bound and gagged, he told us he had sent you here, to this empty building. The girl was never here. See, the superior mind will always triumph over lower forms like you."

He signaled to his minions to come forward and they approached me, keeping clear lines of fire with their guns pointed at me. They had chains in hand.

"You will not resist," Hans ordered. With the gun pressed to Vandoma's head, I had no choice but to let them bind me. They fastened my arms behind me with manacles. I was then led like a lamb to the slaughter into a windowless side room off the stage where I was tied around the waist to a chair with a heavy rope. A wooden chair.

Vandoma and her brother were tied to chairs near me and a single Nazi in full uniform sat at the doorway to the stage keeping his pistol trained on the Roma girl.

"Are you alright, Miss Kalderash?" I whispered in Romani.

She stared at me with pain in her eyes and I could see there were tear tracks on her cheeks. "They came and one of the dogs said you had been hurt so we let them in. They struck Mama and Nico fought them … we could do nothing." She was clearly fighting back tears again.

Nico was sullen, his bruised face and a blackened eye showing he had not been taken prisoner easily.

"I am afraid I must bear you terrible news …."

"Mama?"

"Yes," I said. "She died in my arms. Her last thoughts were for you both."

Nico began to cry quietly, but the news seemed to give new strength to Vandoma, and I saw her straighten up in her chair. Her jaw tightened.

"It is good she was not alone when it came time to pass," she said. "Thank you for being there."

"I'm sorry I brought this on the family Kalderash," I said.

"No." Nico spoke for the first time, his voice hoarse. "It was I who brought this shame and this pain on all. My weakness."

"Such talk does no good, Nico," I said. "This evil would have found its way to us regardless; I now believe such things are fated." Vandoma looked at me and I saw something in her eyes, a deep understanding that she too felt this was a path that was inevitable.

"The *Ursitory* have set this path for us, Mister Paradise," Vandoma said, invoking the three sister fates of the Romani culture. "This is our *baxt*."

"It was my luck that brought this on," Nico said, bitterly.

"No," Vandoma said, "*Sati-Sara* has led us to this that we may stop these beasts who walk as men."

By invoking Saint Sarah, who was the Romani's Goddess of Fate, it was clear to me that Vandoma had prepared herself for anything that might come. As had I, but I was determined that I would find some way to save her and her brother. I had given my word to their mother and though it cost me my own life—which I had lived long and learned much—they had yet to fully live theirs.

"What we have to do now, Nico, is to find a way forward," I said. "Have faith and reason will be our way out."

At that moment Hans entered the ante-room. Behind him on the stage, several robed Nazis were assuming positions for their ritual to come while the auditorium filled with Bundists.

"I hope you are enjoying your last moments, low creatures," he said, his chest swelled with arrogance. "We would have had your Gypsy necklace for maximum effect, but perhaps your impure blood will do as well. In any case, we have two brave, pure-blooded Aryans who will open the portal for us."

"What do you hope to accomplish with this absurdity?" I asked.

Not Born of Woman

"Not *hope*, freak," he said. "*Will* accomplish. We have those talismans of power out there that, with ancient Nordic prayers, will bring the very energy of the old gods down for us. Consecrated in pure blood, we will be able to strike in revenge for the attacks at our rally. We will lead an uprising with the power we gain and cleanse this country of the filth that walks its streets."

"Have you no shame, no conscience?" Vandoma bravely said.

"*Herr* Hitler said that 'Conscience is a Jewish invention,'" Hans replied.

I laughed a cold laugh at him. "Since you like quotes so much, Herr Schmidt, perhaps you're familiar with one by Voltaire. '"Anyone who can make you believe **absurdities** can make you commit atrocities.' Yours are the most absurd of beliefs and what you do in service of them are all atrocities."

His anger made his face red, and I could see he was frustrated he couldn't strike me with his broken arms.

"I will take delight in watching your face as we slit the throat of this bitch before we cut you up as a sacrifice, *Reisen*." He turned and stormed out of the room to the altar and his cohorts.

"I seem to have angered him," I said quietly in Romani. "I can only hope we can inconvenience him considerably more."

CHAPTER TWENTY-NINE

After my sophomoric jibe at the Nazi leader, my attitude sobered, and I applied my intellect to figure out how to extricate us. While on the face it would seem our circumstances were dire, I had come to believe that intellect could overcome brutality and so set myself to discover a way to escape before it was too late.

I was tied to the chair with a rope around my waist and my manacled hands were behind me in such a way that I could not apply any real leverage to even attempt to break free of them.

My legs were free, however. That offered some promise; that and the fact that the chair to which I was secured was an old wooden one. Very little movement caused the chair to creak and that made me optimistic.

Out on the stage, the Nazis, most in ceremonial robes adorned with Nordic runes, chanted in German. They were arrayed around the space like a perverse choir, obviously arranged for effect. The lit incense burners and braziers set about the stage heightened that very dramatic effect. It seemed the theatricality of it all was as important as the actual occult aspect of the ceremony.

Hans presided over the perverse circus, and he stood in a prominent place while red-robed acolytes led two blond Bundists in white robes up to the stage. These two new additions were a man and woman, each no more than twenty and unusually calm—almost as if in a trance with wide staring eyes and placid, almost blank expressions on their faces. The robed Bundists on either side of the stage led the pair to kneel before the altar table, all but carrying them.

Not Born of Woman

I watched the action with keen interest while keeping an eye on our guard whose gaze kept straying from Vandoma to those on stage.

"Brethren," Hans proclaimed in German. "We are gathered here to call forth the powers of the ancient times, to harness the energy of our pure bloodline and bring forth a new *Reich* that will sweep aside the decadent, weak countries that have allowed the master race to be sullied by mixing with lower forms, diluting the purity of the Aryan perfection with mud people and Jews. Your loyalty and strength have enabled us to gather these ancient objects that are filled with the powers of our ancestor's Gods that we will call forth."

He turned to the two white-robed Nazis, gesturing to the handlers on the male. "Joseph and Brunhilde have pledged themselves to our cause and their willing sacrifice of life energy will help us open the pathway to ancient glory. May we all have the dedication and focus they have, to rise to the occasion when we are called on that we may elevate our race to the preeminent position among all the mongrel races, high above the lowly and bestial amalgams that have polluted the world."

He indicated for the man to be made to kneel before him and then another Nazi in a scarlet robe, functioning as "priest," stepped to the altar where they secured the dagger. A second priest took up the chalice. All their movements had the aspect of choreographed drama which I am sure was for the benefit of the rapt Bundist audience.

"What are they going to do?" Vandoma whispered with prescient horror in her tone.

"A savage thing," I replied. "These people are not just calling on ancient powers, they have reverted to the lowest form of humanity."

I saw what was next as plainly as if I had seen their script and said, "Do not look, Vandoma." But my warning was too late.

On the stage the dagger-wielding Bundist stepped before the kneeling man and, after an incantation in ancient German, slowly slid the blade along the throat of the victim, biting deeply into the jugular. Blood poured out in a cascade, pulsing as Joseph's heart continued to pump his life away.

The second priest caught the crimson flow of the blood in the chalice until the cup was full to the brim. By that time, the kneeling

Nazi's head had fallen forward and he was unconscious, held up only by his handlers. As we watched, the gushing blood from his neck ceased to pump, his white robe stained deep brown. His body was pulled away from the altar and set aside on a prepared pyre at the back of the stage which to me felt like he had been left like so much discarded trash. Beside that pyre was a second and it was clear whom it was for.

As the last of his life drained away, an indigo and ebony phantom rose from the corpse, hovering above him by a slender thread of crimson that pulsed and throbbed. The essence of the sacrificed Nazi then rose to ceiling height where it bobbed and shivered like smoke in a strong breeze.

Vandoma gasped and sobbed at the barbarity of what she had seen.

I recalled Voltaire's words again. "Those who can make you believe ***absurdities*** can make you commit atrocities."

These Nazis have no gospel but cruelty and power.

The audience of Nazi thralls cheered at the gory spectacle with some even laughing in a religious ecstasy as if they had witnessed a sacrament, which I suppose to their mind they had.

The sacrificial ceremony was performed again with Brunhilde, the girl also in either a drug- or ecstatic-entranced state. She also showed no reaction as her long blonde hair was pulled back to expose her throat.

I saw people in the audience lean forward, almost licking their lips with hunger and my mind went to what crowds at the Roman Coliseum must have looked like. I wondered why it was I wanted so much to fit in with the species called humans.

As the girl knelt, the priest gave a single deft slice across her throat from ear to ear, this time with the spear point. The blood from her neck was drained into another vessel—what looked to be an elaborately carved golden soup bowl—but which also glowed with its own occult energy. I couldn't begin to guess at its history, nor did I wish to.

The girl's life essence rose to join the other sacrifice, though her phantom was shot through with threads of amber and shards of silver.

Not Born of Woman

The audience again cheered at the horror of the slaughter. I could clearly see couples embracing with sensual delight as if they were watching romantic entertainment. Truly all that was dark in humanity.

All I had to do was look at Vandoma, however, to be reminded that for each shadow there was a light, and I was more determined than ever to find a way out of our dilemma.

While the woman's corpse was placed on her pyre beside the male sacrifice, the leader of the Bund turned to look in our direction with a gleeful grin on his face.

"Now that we have the pure blood to summon the ancient Gods of the Norse," Hans said with a particularly rapturous tone, "we may make the animal sacrifices to show our ancient dead we have triumphed over the base forms and then call down the power to destroy the rest of this mongrel nation."

He looked in our direction and I saw hate in his eyes. "Bring the bitch first!"

"No!" Nico yelled and began to vainly pull against his bonds, screaming until his voice was hoarse. This only seemed to bring joy to Hans and his minions, who all smiled as they entered the small room.

Vandoma remained stoic, though she looked over to me with an expression that showed no fear; instead, it seemed to have confidence in it. Confidence in fate.

It was my moment to be the agent of that fate.

As one of the robed acolytes passed me, I kicked out with my right foot to snap his lead leg at the shin so that he fell over with a scream of agony. As he fell over onto me, I planted my feet on the floor to partially rise and then slammed myself down hard. Our combined weight and the force of my dropping at an angle on the chair legs had enough violence to shatter the chair I was bound to. I slammed to the floor on my hands and back.

There was a lance of pain in my side where I had been shot and my weight on my hands hurt but I could feel the chair fall apart beneath me, so my strategy had worked.

The second acolyte reacted slowly, which gave me the moment I needed to heave the maimed Nazi off me. I wiggled to disentangle myself from the remnants of the chair then rolled onto my back and pulled my knees to my chest, allowing me to get my manacled hands in front of me.

By now the guard at the opening of the room, who had moved to allow the acolytes to pass, raised his gun to fire. I gained my feet, grabbed the second acolyte who was standing with a confused expression on his face, and flung him with all my might into the gunman.

Both Nazis flew out of the side room with considerable velocity where they slammed into the altar. Their bodies knocked the altar over and the sanguine contents of the full vessels, that the sacrifices had so dearly paid for, splashed out to stain the altar cloth and stage.

Hans screamed incoherently and the Bundists in the auditorium began to cry out in confusion, as they had not seen the interaction in the side room, only the bodies flying out.

I immediately ripped apart the ropes that bound the Kalderash siblings and then spun, holding the chair to which Nico had been bound before me as a weapon.

"Say behind me," I called. "They will reorganize in moments; this may be pointless—"

"But we must make their victory cost," Vandoma said with vehemence and not a jot of fear. She held a leg of my crushed chair like a club. I felt deeply proud to stand with her.

Before I could charge out of the doorway to the stage there was a new element added to the chaos. A sudden series of loud booming noises filled the auditorium and, in a moment, I realized it was the storm shutters that were slamming shut with a series of metallic clangs.

"The door, my God, what is it? Look!" A woman's voice cried out shrilly in the pandemonium of voices and all eyes turned from the stage toward the main door to the room.

Even Hans looked and I saw him freeze in what I can only describe as horror.

Then I saw where he was looking and what he was looking at.

Standing just inside the double doors was a sight out of some primordial nightmare.

It was a bipedal thing, some nine feet in height, dark grey and ruddy brown. It was roughly in the shape of a man, but more of a blank template of mankind, with the vaguest of features that only implied eyes, nose, and mouth. It appeared like a rough form of a moving statue for it looked to be made of clay!

And one more thing—there, around the neck of the creature was the *Koshti Bok* of the Kalderash family! The necklace glowed a bright scarlet, pulsing in an occult aura that I was sure only I could see.

I knew then that I was looking at a thing out of legend, a creature fashioned out of clay and earth. I was looking at a golem!

CHAPTER THIRTY

Several guards in militarist uniforms moved to grapple with the nightmare figure but with an unholy roar the golem struck out at the first two to reach it, its blockish fists smashing into and crushing the skulls of both men.

As I watched, the figure moved forward into the group of Bundists and began to lay about the crowd with great clubbing blows, felling men and women with equal violence. Several of the armed Nazis aimed their Tommy guns at the creature but were clearly reluctant to fire for fear of hitting their own compatriots.

"Shoot it, you fools!" Hans screamed in near apoplectic fury, "Kill it before it kills us all."

This decided the gunmen and they began to spray bullets at the clay behemoth, but the forty-five caliber slugs ripped into the creature, chipping off small stone pieces and tearing off small chunks of the rock-like apparition to no apparent effect.

Some of the Bundists tried to flee by smashing chairs against the windows but the storm shutters were firmly fastened on the outside and held in place by metal bars against any hurricane. It was clear that someone had deliberately confined the Nazis in the room to create a killing ground for the primordial monster.

Vandoma, Nico, and I were trapped in that abattoir along with the Nazis.

The golem moved with mechanical precision through the ranks of the Bundists with horrific violence, each blow of its rock-like fists felling one of the uniformed Nazis. Some of the people the golem grabbed by their clothing and flung into others, some it threw directly into the walls where they collided with force enough to leave bloody smudges where they struck.

The black phantoms of the dead rose from the newly murdered like a squall of storm clouds and all but obscured the living forms that raced around the room in terror before me.

Hans and his compatriots on the stage had all but forgotten us, the greater terror of the golem and the slaughter occurring in the room keeping all their attention.

All this occurred in fewer than a hundred heartbeats. Nico used this distraction to dive across the stage and snatch up the pistol that our doorway guard had dropped. He rose with the weapon in his hand but with no clear focus as his target.

"Nico," I called, "stay back here in the room." When he looked at me, I indicated Vandoma. "Stay with your sister." He looked to argue for a moment but the carnage in the auditorium became even more violent, accompanied by deafening screams. He seemed to realize there was no escape that way.

It seemed to me that the best chance of survival for the siblings would be to fort up in the side room while the terror out front ran its course.

The Roma came back behind me even as Hans recovered enough from his shock to turn his furious gaze on me.

"You, *Reisen*," he screamed, "you have done this!" He pointed at me with one of his broken arms and two of the acolytes on the stage decided I was the lesser of two opponents, so they charged at me.

I was in no mood to mitigate my wrath so when the first robed thug reached me, I clubbed him in the face with my right fist. The blow had all my anger behind it and caved his cheek in a bloody mess. The second Bundist I grabbed by the robe, sending him to collide with some of his companions. They all fell to the stage by the bodies of their fellows at Hans' feet.

"You have destroyed all chance of summoning the ancient power," Hans yelled hysterically, "and brought this monster on us!" He came at me with madness in his eyes, though what he intended to do with his arms in casts I do not know.

I was done with his strident fanaticism, so I picked him up and threw him into the middle of the chaos in the auditorium. Hans' screams blended with the others but rose in volume when the golem grabbed him, raised him over its head, and literally snapped him in half with a cascade of blood and intestines.

"Mister Paradise!" Vandoma called to me from the side room where her brother was physically trying to block her from exiting. Bullets from the guns of the Nazis still passed through the golem, many of the lead slugs wounding or killing their own people. Some of the slugs even buzzed in the direction of the stage, kicking up splinters of wood.

"Stay back, Vandoma," I said. "Stay behind that wall."

I grabbed the table-cum-altar and cleared off all of the religious objects and the altar cloth. I pulled it over to the entrance to the side room. There I upended the table and put it in place of a doorway as a barrier. It was not much protection, but I hoped it might help.

The golem continued to rampage through the Bundists. Many of the trapped people had finally realized that the windows and doors were all sealed so had turned to attack the beast with chairs and any other weapons they could find in desperation.

The creature did not seem to care what was used on it, even when pieces of the granite hard clay that composed it were chipped off. It moved relentlessly throughout the entire room, smashing, tearing, and tossing about everyone it encountered.

The screams and sobs of the Nazis, male and female were a continuous shriek like the wails of tormented souls in hell. There was sporadic gunfire still, but most of those with guns had spent most of their ammunition to no effect.

The floor of the auditorium was a mass of flesh and gore. The clay creature continued to walk over the corpses, each step grinding bodies to unrecognizable pulp.

Some who had fallen were still alive but when the golem passed by them as it circled the room on the hunt for more victims, it smashed a massive foot down on them and they were stilled forever.

Not Born of Woman

A few of the Nazis, seeing no other refuge, climbed out of the slaughter to the stage but there was no outlet there save into the side room where the Kalderashes were holed up.

I stood in front of the upended table/altar and was forced to repel the frantic survivors. There was no reasoning with the desperate Bundists who charged at me with fear-driven madness in their eyes.

The first Nazi that came at me screaming was a man in his twenties. He swung a chair at my head. I ducked and accepted the chair blow on my left arm, then yanked it from him and flung it aside.

"Go!" I snarled. I had no desire to add to the carnage of the room, but I would not let anyone endanger the two behind me and so I was the Cerberus at the gate.

The panicked Nazi came at me again and so I had no choice but to stop him. I grabbed his shoulders as he tried to pummel me with his fists and lifted him bodily to fling him back onto the auditorium floor. He screamed in terror as he fell on a pile of bloody corpses.

He was still screaming when the golem turned to stomp a massive foot down on his head, crushing it like a ripe melon.

Two more of the frantic Bundists, a man and a woman, tried to overwhelm me with a simultaneous attack but I would not budge. I slapped the man down and grabbed the woman by her shirt.

"Stop," I commanded. "Stop now." I shook her to try and get her to listen to me. "Come to your senses."

"Get out of my way, you Jewish freak," she screamed at me.

My patience was at an end with the delusions of these Nazis, so I slapped her with an open hand to render her unconscious. She dropped at my feet.

The screams in the hall had died to whimpers of the surviving fallen with only a dozen or so of the almost one hundred Bundists still on their feet. They had all moved to the back of the room and were frantically trying to get the doors open, though with no success.

The golem moved methodically across the room purposely stepping on any of the living fallen it came across and grinding the life out of them. It moved to the last standing Nazis with inexorable and deliberate steps. Its arms were wide almost as if to embrace them.

One of the survivors was Gunther from the pawnshop. As the clay creature approached him, he cursed and pushed one of his own compatriots at the golem. The creature, which was now stained a ruddy brown with the blood that covered it, merely brought its hands together as if clapping and crushed the skull of the Bundist to paste.

This action brought a scream of terror from Gunther who turned to claw at the door while whimpering and crying.

The golem methodically clubbed each of the standing Nazis down now, finally putting one massive claw-like hand on Gunther's head and grabbing him by the uniform belt. Then with one sickening sucking sound and a final pop, he tore the Nazi's head from his body.

The golem then turned and paused as if surveying the carnage it had wrought. Spread out before it was a scene as if from a battlefield of yore with dismembered and broken forms from wall to wall.

The creature's face, though roughly cast in a human form, had cheeks, mouth, nose, and brow but no eyes, merely indentations that were in deep shadow. Regardless, I felt as if it was looking over its handy work, and then, with a deliberate motion, it raised its head to look directly toward me.

There was a frozen moment where I looked at the death dealer through the clouds of the black and crimson phantoms of the slaughtered Nazis that filled the room and it looked back.

Then with slow, deliberate steps, the golem moved across the room straight for me.

CHAPTER THIRTY-ONE

The golem lumbered toward me, its footfalls muffled as it stepped in the gore of the dead and dying Bundists.

"What is happening, Mister Paradise?" Vandoma called from behind the makeshift barrier of the table.

"Stay hidden, both of you," I said in Romani. "Whatever happens to me, stay there."

"No, Mister Paradise we—" she said.

"Please, Vandoma," I said, "This is why I am here—that you may live. It may not find you both there. I will try to distract it enough so you may be able to escape if you stay there."

"No," she said stepping out from behind the barrier. "This is not a thing you will do." She looked at the hall covered in blood and bodies and shivered in revulsion. The golem continued its slow walk toward us as if it sensed we had nowhere to go. "You are here for us, and we Kalderash do not hide."

"Yes," Nico said. "We do not leave our friends in danger."

I was touched by both their words, especially her brother's considering our history.

"Please stay back," I pleaded. "I fear there is nothing you can do."

"That is our *Kushti Bok*," Vandoma gasped, looking at the necklace on the creature. Her voice was not quivering with fear as I would expect but had a tinge of anger. This was a remarkable person. "It has been used for this evil."

"Yes," I said, "to bring forth this creature and I think for the very purpose of killing these Nazis."

Nico raised his pistol to point it at the golem, but I stayed his hand. "It will do no good, Nico. Now, please go back and hide; I can only hope to injure it or draw it away; that is all."

I chanced a glance at Vandoma and saw that she was near tears. "No, Mister Paradise. You must not."

Before I could continue to argue with her there came a sound from the back of the room. The doors were yanked open!

"In here, Captain," a voice called, followed by, "*oh my God!*"

Armed and uniformed State Troopers had forced the doors to the auditorium open and half a dozen of them stopped, stunned by the hideous carnage in the room. Tommy Shane stepped past the lead trooper and froze.

"What in the name of God has gone on in here?" Tommy said.

The golem stopped moving.

"Get back, Tommy, that thing is unstoppable," I yelled.

For a long moment, it stood still while the state troopers filled the doorway, some of them racking their shotguns.

Then the creature turned.

"Halt right there," one of the uniforms called with a desperate tone that was almost pathetic. "You're under arrest."

The golem moved toward the new interlopers with a steady lumbering gait, arms outstretched as if coming to embrace them.

"Get back," I called to Vandoma and Nico. I pushed them back into the side room just as the state troopers opened fire on the clay behemoth. The shotgun slugs tore into the walking nightmare, chipping off bits of stony clay but none of the fusillades stopped the simulacrum's progress.

I pushed the Kalderashes behind the wall into the side room just as the pellets from the shotguns cut into the presidium of the stage.

The sounds of the firing were disrupted by curses and yells of pain. I imagined the golem repeating his assault as he had on the Nazis and thought that they would have just as much luck against the occult-powered behemoth.

That's it! I suddenly realized. *Occult powered!*

"Please, Vandoma," I said to her as I pressed her against the back wall of the small room. "Stay here, I know now what I must do." The look in her eyes made me pause and then add, "I just had an idea that might work out. I promise I will come back."

I didn't give her a chance to answer and turned to run out onto the stage to a new circus of chaos in the auditorium. The golem had reached the lawmen and was smashing and throttling them with the same ruthlessness it had used on the Nazis.

"The guns are useless," I cried as I leapt from the stage and ran across the charnel house floor at the golem. "Let me handle it."

I was not being glib or noble. It had occurred to me that the red glow I saw on the *Koshti Bok* was the key. If someone had killed all those girls to find the power to create such a creature—and since that creature was wearing the necklace of the Kalderash—then that necklace was integral to its creation.

The troopers had stopped shooting for the most part because they feared hitting their fellows, some of whom the golem was savaging.

Tommy was armed with only his police special and was taking careful aim, placing targeted shots into the empty eye sockets of the creature.

"Get back, Tommy," I yelled as I ran. "I think the necklace is the key to stopping it." At my voice, the clay Goliath threw down the state trooper it had just killed and turned to face me with surprising speed.

I had no time to stop or dodge aside so I sped up and jumped to collide with the chest of the creature, its arms encircling me. I managed to keep my own arms up and free above the massive, rock hard, clay pincers that squeezed in on my ribs hard enough to take my breath away.

"Jeeze, Adam, no!" Tommy yelled.

"No," I heard Vandoma scream, despite my admonition to stay hidden.

I was being crushed in the arms with enough force that I felt my ribs straining, the power even greater than the polar bear I'd fought so long ago. Pressed as I was into the clay chest that was as hard as concrete, I could smell the ripe scent of earth and death that hung about it, a mix of blood and gore and a deeper smell of something beyond even my experience.

The face of it was horrid close up, the hollow eye sockets more frightening than if it had seeing orbs. Above, on the forehead of the creature was a glyph etched in Hebrew letters. There was no breath from the line that marked its mouth and I realized abruptly that it did not respirate as I did for it was not alive at all. Perhaps that was my difference from it.

I also felt the tingle from the necklace it wore, a warmth that came with the deep red glow that I knew only I saw. I reached over the head with my manacled arms so that my hands were behind the massive neck and fumbled for the catch on the *Koshti Bok*. I raced to find the release before it throttled me into unconsciousness.

I had not realized my gloves would make my already clumsy fingers even worse and the simple act of unhooking the necklace became nearly impossible. I could not even dig into the rock-hard clay around the necklace to gain any purchase.

I was aware suddenly that the golem was making a low rumbling sound, almost at the lower edge of hearing. It was like distant thunder heard from a deep hole.

There were also shouts I was distantly aware of as well, Vandoma screaming, troopers yelling, and Tommy whose voice clearly said, "Adam, Adam, get out of the way."

My vision began to swim and redden, and I was not able to draw another breath within the compressing arms. I realized I had to act before it was too late.

I gave up trying to pull the catch free, simply grabbed the edges of the necklace, and pulled with all my remaining strength.

The metal of the latch gave way. I yanked the necklace from around the neck of the golem and tossed it to the floor.

The golem roared now at full volume. A hot, earthy smell flowed over me from its mouth, but the arms did not release. Instead, they tightened even more. I felt my ribs crack.

No, it hasn't worked.

I fell back on my instincts then and clawed at the clay of the back, but this time I felt my fingers dig into the oily surface leaving deep gouges. It had suddenly softened with the removal of the necklace.

"Shoot now," I gasped out. "It will be vulnerable now."

Not Born of Woman

"No," Tommy called. "We'll hit you."

"Do it," I yelled as another rib cracked. "You have to forget me."

"No," Tommy answered.

One of his trooper companions, however, did not take his order. A shot rang out and the golem jerked in reaction.

It is vulnerable now!

"Keep shooting," I moaned. Red lights swam before my eyes and I thought that this time, perhaps when I closed them, it would be for the last time.

I clawed at the neck and shoulders of the creature as I began to lose consciousness, hanging off the creature like a necklace myself. I was literally tearing away chunks of the body with my clawing fingers. The behemoth began to stumble but when I felt it tighten its arms again this time, despite the biceps being of softer clay, the pressure of them was a vice.

Distantly, I heard Vandoma yell, "No!" and a red haze fell over me.

Then in the crimson darkness, a golden glow grew from a pinpoint and a figure floated down to hover before me. Mother Kalderash, in phantom form, was behind the golem and looking at me.

"Mother Kalderash," I said, "I need to save Vandoma."

"*One called Adam,*" her phantom said, "*remember that the truth is the path to salvation.*"

"I don't understand," I said. "I think I will join you now; I have long wondered if there was somewhere for me after—"

"*Truth,*" she said again. "*In truth is salvation.*"

And abruptly I knew what she meant, what she had meant back at her home.

I reached my arms up and over the head and put my left hand to the now soft clay of its forehead. There I wiped the first letter from the Hebrew glyph on the golem's forehead that said "truth," which changed the word to "death."

The creature shuddered and suddenly the arms confining me went slack. I fell from its grip to land among the gory remains of the Bundists.

I hit the floor with a wet sound so that I was looking up at the towering creature. Now it swayed back and forth, the very illusion of life gone from it, nothing more than a crude statue. Above the former golem floated the golden, ghostly figure of Mother Kalderash.

There was a sound like a rushing wind as the golem stopped moving. It crumbled to pieces and fell over on top of me like a cascade of wet mud.

The last thing I saw was the old Roma woman's ghost smiling down at me as she faded away toward the ceiling. Then I was wrapped in blackness that I was sure would be eternal.

CHAPTER THIRTY-TWO

Carl Jung said, "There is no coming to consciousness without pain," but when my eyes first opened so long ago in the laboratory of Victor Frankenstein, there was no immediate pain. Then I knew nothing of the conscious world; what I knew was only the face before me—the sallow, wide-eyed face of my creator. He was the first living being I saw and when he shunned me it ultimately drove me from civilization because I felt as if I was a mistake, an aberration that did not deserve to have the gift of life.

I even tried to take my own life, albeit in a passive way, by heading into the bitter cold of the arctic. Yet life, that force, that spark within me that Victor had somehow awakened, was a fire that would not be snuffed out. I survived every vicissitude over my many years alone, all in a quest for some meaning, of some sign that I had a purpose in the universe.

Descartes said, "I think therefore I am," but is mere existence enough? Should a being not also have purpose? The reason I returned to the world of mankind was to find that purpose. And when a simple Roma woman came to me for help to recover a family heirloom, I found it.

So, it was right that when I opened my eyes after the golem had fallen on me it was Vandoma's worried face that I saw.

"Adam Paradise," she said in Romani, "it is good you are back with us."

Behind her, I saw her brother and Tommy Shane.

I was in the hallway outside the Camp Siegfried auditorium on a stretcher while dozens of uniformed police and hospital personnel swarmed past me.

"We thought we lost you, big guy," Tommy said. His features were drawn, and his normally immaculate suit covered with grime and blood. "We had a hell of a time clearing that clay thing off you. You've been out cold for almost an hour."

I looked down to see my chest was bare and my wounded side had been re-bandaged.

"You did not tell us you had been shot before," Vandoma said with a little anger in her tone.

"It wasn't bad," I lied. Moving, even speaking hurt my side.

I must have grimaced because Tommy said, "The doctor thinks you have broken ribs, so you're going to the hospital to get a proper working over, but they're taking the more serious cases first."

"How bad?" I asked.

"We haven't finished a count," Tommy said. "Four state troopers dead, five badly hurt, and two of my guys hurt but walking wounded."

"Any of the Nazis survive?"

"So far, we found only ten still breathing but it's a mess in there. And some of them are in very bad shape." He looked a little sick. "What the hell happened in there, Adam?"

"We told the policeman that the Nazi men took us—" Vandoma said.

"And they were going to sacrifice us," Nico added. "They even killed their own people."

"I told them I was there at their house," Tommy said. "And they filled me in on the event here. I believe them but what I want to know is, what does this all mean? What the hell were these Bundists trying to do?"

"I can only guess, Tommy. They were after all the occult objects to give them some sort of special powers to become supermen."

"You're telling me that all that blood and death was because they were trying to become some funny book characters?"

Not Born of Woman

"I didn't say it made sense," I said. "Then someone—I have to think whoever killed those girls in New York created that golem you saw, to kill the Nazis."

"That 'thing' ..." he said, shaking his head. "I saw it and I still don't believe it. How am I gonna explain that in a report?"

"'There are more things in heaven and Earth, Horatio, Than are dreamt of in your philosophy,'" I quoted. I would have laughed at myself for doing so, but with my side, I thought better of it. "I recommend you think of a good lie and get your people to swear to it."

"I've been thinking that," he said almost absentmindedly. "Now you just rest and listen to the doctors, Adam. I have to take charge of this, but you'll get a visit for a full statement in a day or so."

"I will go with you, Adam Paradise," Vandoma said. It was a hard and fast statement, and I didn't feel a bit like arguing. "Nico will go now to begin things for Mother's funeral."

"And my deepest condolences to both of you about your mother," Tommy said to the siblings. I saw both of them register his sincerity in this and they acknowledged it with solemn nods.

"Our *Koshti Bok*," Nico asked. "It is ours. It should be at the sending away of our mother."

Tommy and I exchanged a look.

"It is a religious object to them, Tommy."

He hesitated for a moment. "I have to book it into evidence," he said. "It was involved in this. I will sign it out to you for the funeral, but you'll have to put it back into evidence afterward. If that's okay."

The two siblings looked undecided for a long minute then they nodded.

"It is good," Nico said. "We understand this. Thank you."

"You rest now, Adam Paradise," Vandoma said. "I will make sure all is well."

"I think you will, Vandoma," I said and closed my eyes. "I think you will."

I was supposed to be taken to a local hospital to be X-rayed and have my bullet wound stitched properly but I persuaded—with a promise of money—the ambulance driver to take me all the way to New York City and St. Vincent's Hospital.

Nico rode with us and we three were silent most of the trip. I'm sure the enormity of the horror they had seen weighed heavily on the siblings. For my part, I played over the events of the day and all that had come before, trying to parse out everything.

Had the Nazis really thought they would gain powers or was Hans playing to their superstitions to bind them to him by complicity in the deaths? And it's clear that someone else had taken the Koshti Bok to create the golem. And that person killed the girls. So, this is not over ... not at all.

At St. Vincent's, I was admitted while Nico left—with a note from Tommy to aid in getting the release of his mother's body to begin arranging her funeral. I could not convince Vandoma to leave me.

"I do not trust *gadjo* places," she said. "My mother was a healer; I know something of this. I will watch them."

"Like a hawk, little mother," I joked. When she looked at me with a side-eye as I said it, I added, "and I am glad for your eagle eyes."

It happened that I had three fractured ribs, so there was not much they could do but tape me up and advise that I take to bed for a day or more. My bullet wound they were more concerned about, if for no other reason than because all bullet wounds had to be reported to the police. Fortunately, Tommy had covered that as well and had called ahead to let the staff know that I had gotten the wound "in the line of duty" or some such and so they cleaned and sewed up the wound without more than the usual paperwork.

As we were preparing to leave the hospital a male nurse walked up to me.

"Adam?" Daniel said with surprise. "What did you do to yourself this time?"

"I just had a little mishap with a lump of clay."

"Okay, don't tell me." He said, "But I'll stop by when I get off duty to check up on you."

Vandoma took a moment then registered that it was the same person she had met as Dottie and smiled. "Hello—"

"Daniel, here, dearie," they said with an answering smile. "It's good to see you again."

"And you," she said.

"Maybe I shouldn't stop by later, then," Daniel said with a slight leer.

"He will welcome it," Vandoma said, reclaiming propriety. "This eagle eye will go home to help my brother. It was nice to meet you again."

"I'll come over tomorrow when I wake up, Daniel," I said. "I think I need sleep more than anything."

"Pleasant dreams then, you big hunk," they said. "I'll make extra coffee in the morning."

Vandoma accompanied me to my apartment a block away and insisted on coming with me to make sure I was safe and sound in my room before she went home. I made her promise to take a taxicab. She also insisted on being the one to lean down to check the hair across the doorjamb to see that it was untouched, so I did not have to bend.

"I'm really okay," I said in protest. "I heal fast." She simply ignored me, checked, and then stood.

"It is still there," she said. "Now I can go."

"You *will* take that taxi?"

"Yes," she said, "I have promised."

"Good," I said. "And please don't worry. I'll recover—this is not so serious as it seems. I'll call tomorrow so I may know when the ... the ceremony for your mother is."

We stood for a moment in uncomfortable silence.

Finally, I said, "I'm sorry that I could not be there to save your mother."

"But you were there so she did not die alone—or with a stranger," she said. "This matters. And you have returned the *Koshti Bok* to the family Kalderash. You have done what you promised, and I will begin to shop for your dinner after my mother is sent on her journey."

"There's no rush for that; my hunger isn't going anywhere. Good night, Vandoma Kalderash."

"Good night, Adam Paradise," she replied. "Sleep in peace."

I entered my studio, locking the door behind me but going immediately to the window, watching until she exited my building and caught a cab on the corner of Eight Avenue. That allowed me to relax.

I took off my filthy, bloody clothes, throwing them in a pile to be disposed of, and stood naked in the center of the room, staring out at the Empire State Building. It was a dark shape this late at night, lit only by ambient light from the rest of Manhattan.

I was struck with the fancy that it resembled nothing so much as a large headstone, reminding me that there had been so much death in the past weeks. The Nazis, the pawnbrokers, the girls that were killed … and Mother Kalderash.

This is not done.

I lay down on the bed and was asleep in moments. Thankfully, it was a deep and dreamless sleep.

CHAPTER THIRTY-THREE

I attended the funeral of Mother Kalderash four days later. There were several hundred Romani from many states around that came to wish the respected elder a bon voyage.

I did my best to remain unobtrusive, but Vandoma insisted on introducing me to many of her clan, who, unaware that I spoke their language had some interesting things to say about the "tall *gadjo* with the scars." I think Vandoma enjoyed knowing I understood, a shared secret. She wore the *Koshti Bok* at her neck over a black dress.

Afterward, we stood outside the cemetery.

"It is good you came to be here, Adam Paradise. I think mother will look down on this with joy."

"I know she does, Vandoma."

"I will come to the office tomorrow to get my typewriter," she said. "And we will talk of when you wish your dinner."

"Not come to type?"

"There is no reason to come there to type. I can type at home."

"But is it not more convenient to pick up and drop off typing from my address?" I asked. "And I've been thinking of getting a telephone myself. It would not be bad to have someone on hand to answer the phone. You would still be able to do your typing most of the time."

Her expression flowed from stoic to confused and then after a moment morphed into a gentle smile. "I will bring work tomorrow, Mister Paradise."

"I will see you then, Miss Kalderash."

I went back to my office, picking up a paper on the way. The front page still had the "facts" of the "Slaughter at Siegfried" as the powers that be in city and state government dictated it—the official story was a war between factions of the Bund. All the police had been sworn to secrecy and, in truth, most of them had no coherent way to really describe what they had seen and experienced so were just as happy to block it from their collective memories.

There was a second article on the young girls that had been killed, with school photos of all of them, I suppose to tug at the heartstrings of the public. It did not connect the killings to the Long Island deaths and, hopefully, would not. After all, the two seemed worlds apart; only a few of us knew how they were connected. As I looked at the photos of the young girls whose lives had been snuffed out for a twisted agenda, I saw something.

No, it can't be!

Yet the longer I looked at one particular photo the more certain I was of what I saw. And it saddened me.

"How are you, Adam?" Mort asked as I entered his drug store. He was, as usual, straightening up the pharmacy area. Jake was cleaning the counter by the soda fountain.

"Hey, Mister P!" Jake called. "You ain't been around for a couple of days. Been busy?"

"A little," I said. My ribs had healed enough so that I showed no gingerness in my steps but I chose to lean on the pharmacy counter so I could lower my voice in speaking to Mort.

"What is it, Adam?" Mort said. "You look so serious."

Not Born of Woman

Since I had picked up the paper, I had dreaded how I was going to broach the topic with a man I had come to call a friend. Now that I was there with him, I had no real method decided on, so I simply said, "Why, Mort, why?" I set the paper down on the counter with the "Siegfried Slaughter" headline.

My friend put down the boxes he was arranging and looked at the paper, then up at me in surprise. At first, I thought he would play coy and try to deny things, but then he smiled in a way I had never seen from him.

"I was concerned when you didn't come to work for several days," Mort said. "I was afraid that you might have been at that camp."

"I was, Mort."

"Then you saw—" His eyes went from mine to look past me at Jake and I thought I detected fear in them.

"No, Mort, I did not see—I experienced. How could you unleash such a hideous thing?"

"You know what monsters those Nazis are," Mort said bitterly. He came to stand directly on the other side of the counter, looking up at me with an inner fire in his eyes. "They killed my sister in Germany on *Krystalnacht*. You saw that no one in that country or this one will oppose them. Instead, here they celebrate them at parties at Madison Square Garden. They let them open summer camps for children!" His voice was shrill, his manner completely different than the man I knew. "They are devils on earth and must be driven from it."

"You cannot realize what a horror you created—the death you have caused," I said. "What you have unleashed with that monster—"

"You have the temerity to speak of that." His mouth curled up in a sneer. "When you are an abomination in the eyes of God who would hide yourself among us?"

"You know?" I gasped.

His words stung me like a lash. I suddenly felt as if nothing I had learned in my time among men meant anything. The revulsion I felt when my creator had shunned me came back on me and I felt abruptly lost again.

"Not from the first," Mort said. "When you rented that office from me, I was beginning my studies to create *der* golem for I sensed what the National Socialists would become—but one night I stumbled on your journal when I was curious about my new tenant who seemed so unusual. While I was appalled at first, I came to consider it a gift from God—a sign that what I was seeking to do was possible. Just as when I found mention of the Gypsy necklace in a manuscript and quietly put out the word to pawnshops that I was looking for it. It was really a gift to find it, though it took some work for my protégé to get it."

"And Dorfman was fun, he squealed like a pig on a spit." Jake spoke from behind me, and I spun to see he had locked the door and stood holding a semi-automatic pistol—a Mauser—pointed at me.

"Jake," I said. "You too?"

"You can call me Jack." The young red-haired boy was as I had never seen him, his features twisted into a mask of hate, even madness. Moreover, the grey phantoms I had seen hover near him were now multiplied by a dozen shapes and were jagged black and crimson forms that told the story of great violence following him.

"Jake—" I began.

"Jack!" he spat out. "Not that weakling. He could never do what I do—he doesn't have the courage."

The boy was so completely different in manner, voice, and actions he might as well have been a separate individual. Whatever twist in his psyche existed, it was so complete a split in personality that his very soul was compartmented. Jake was an innocent boy, somehow completely partitioned from the Jack persona. A true Jekyll and Hyde, though I had seen a glimmer of that other self in his eyes when he saved me from the hooligans with the seltzer bottle.

"It is unfortunate you discovered what we did," Mort said after a moment, his voice low. He seemed truly sad. "But I can't help but wonder how?"

"Little things that I wasn't even aware of at first," I said. I was very conscious of the boy behind me with the gun pointed at my back but also knew he was well out of arm's reach. "I realized you had to have been the one looking at my *Amuletae boni et mali* when I considered who could have access. When I thought back on it, I should have realized when I found you in the back office that night. You also seemed to be even more versed in the passages I brought you than an average scholar should have been—unless you had also made a study of the occult. Still, none of it came to clarity until I saw the photo of the girl in the paper today. That is when I put it all together."

"Girl?"

"Rebecca Gartz," I said. "I remembered when I saw her picture today that I had seen that redhead before, here, flirting with Jake."

The boy laughed. "Jake has a talent for finding them," he said. "Becky was a real laugh—he used her to get to the pawnbroker. Then I took it from there." His twisted smile widened, and his comment chilled me. "That was a fun pair."

"I worried it was too much of a risk with her," Mort said. "But when she proved to be at the Gartz home, it was a good way to send the police off looking in another direction. There seemed to be no choice."

"Her blood was the last we needed," the boy said.

"Yes," Mort said with regret I felt was feigned, "That life-giving liquid had to be mixed with the clay to imbue it with the semblance of life."

"It gave us the last of the power we needed to raise the clay guy," Jack giggled.

"Why did you have to kill the priest and the others?" I asked, though, sadly my guess on that was proven true when he spoke.

"That weakling Jake actually went to confession after I had fun with Dorfman. He remembered some—enough to cause me trouble," Jack said. "I had to shut him up."

"And they let you in as a delivery boy."

"Yeah," he laughed. "That was a good one; the priest begged and begged."

I felt sick to my stomach.

"You have to be stopped," I said.

"What can you do, monster?" Mort said with a cold laugh. "You do not have the heart for action. Nothing to stop us. It will take a longer time to create another, but we will."

"Create another?" I asked. "You think I'll let you get away with that horror again?"

"Your morals will not let you strike out at us; I know this of you. I will recreate my golem and he will rise as a protector to my people and destroy all those who would persecute the holy and the chosen. I will find a replacement for the Gypsy necklace, some other item to keep the clay of his being strong and solid."

"Do you hear yourself? The hypocrisy of it? You are speaking like the very people you purport to hate."

"How dare you accuse me of that, you blight in God's eye?"

I felt as if I had been lanced in the side, yet how could I argue? My own creator had thought me an aberration and failure. Was I so different from the clay behemoth from the Nazi camp?

Yes, I can feel pain in my heart.

"I will find a way to stop you."

"No, you won't, freak," Jack said. I heard him cock the gun.

"No need, Jack," Mort said. "His death here would just bring attention. He will do nothing. He will slink away to another life under another name or else risk being exposed and destroyed. It is all he can do. Though I am sorry for your going, Adam—I enjoyed our conversations, even when I finally knew what you were."

I looked from him to the boy and realized he was right. I could not raise my hand against these two whom I had called friends. And I could not bear the light of exposure.

"I say this to you, Mort," I said as I walked to the door and unlocked it. Then I quoted Nietzsche, "'Whoever fights monsters should see to it that in the process he does not become a monster. And if you gaze long enough into an abyss, the abyss will gaze back into you.'"

As I left the store, I thought about all Mort had said and all he had done. Yes, he was right to want to protect his people from the hate of the Nazis, but in doing so he had become as evil as they.

I thought about the forces that had brought me into this drama, about meeting and befriending Tommy Shane, then Vandoma and the necklace. And the happenstance that brought me to rent the office over Mort's drug store the year before.

So much of that seemed random yet now I saw it as the hand of Fate, of a grander scheme that had brought me back to this time and

Not Born of Woman

this place. One that allowed me to see not just the evil of the Nazis and Mort—but the good of Vandoma, Tommy, and Mother Kalderash.

I could not allow Mort to take more lives and this time I would not run; I had found a place for myself. I could have a purpose and make a difference in the world. I would have to act though I knew I would feel sick for what I must do.

I recalled the words of the devil in Paradise Lost: "Did I request thee, Maker, from my clay to mould me man? Did I solicit thee from darkness to promote me?"

I walked a block to a diner where I went into a phone booth and placed a call.

"Mister Manzetti," I said with a quiver in my voice, "I have two names for you as I promised. You should probably take care of the matter soon …."

After I hung up, I went to see the movie of *Hound of the Baskervilles* with Basil Rathbone where everything was in black and white, and I could be sure that all the monsters were human, and the good guys won.

"He was soon borne away by the waves and lost in darkness and distance."

Mary Wollstonecraft Shelley

ABOUT THE AUTHOR

Teel James Glenn traveled the world for forty-plus years as a stuntman, swordmaster, storyteller, bodyguard, actor, and haunted house barker before turning to writing.

He has several dozen novels published and his novel *A Cowboy in Carpathia: A Bob Howard Adventure* won best novel 2021 in the Pulp Factory Award. He is also the winner of the 2012 Pulp Ark Award for Best Author.

His short stories have been printed in over two hundred magazines including *Weird Tales, Mystery, Pulp Adventures, Cirsova, Silverblade, Heroic Fantasy, Blazing Adventures* and *Sherlock Holmes Mystery*.

His website is: TheUrbanSwashbuckler.com
Facebook: Teel James Glenn
Bsky: @Teelglenn

Bibliography

Novels and Novellas
A Cowboy in Carpathia
A Year of Shadows
Bayou Sinistre
Bloodstone Confidential

Britannia Occultus
Callback for a Corpse
Chronicles of the Skullmask
Cultists Always Ring Twice
Deadly Shadows
Dragonthroat
Fae Well, My Lovely
Fear the Reaper
Gaslight Magick
Ghostmaker Inc.
Journey to Stormrest
Killing Shadows
Not Born of Woman
Semper Occultus
The Clockwork Nutcracker
The Cowboy & The Conqueror
The Cowboy and the Contest

Curious about other Crossroad Press books? Stop by our website:
http://crossroadpress.com
We offer quality writing
in digital, audio, and print formats.

Subscribe to our newsletter on the website homepage and receive a free eBook.

Made in United States
North Haven, CT
12 November 2024